"Are you allowed to kiss me good-bye?"

"Just one little kiss?" she [...]

The despairing look in [...]
so, under the circumsta[...]
isn't the setting I'd pl[...]
have to do."

Circling the desk, he pulled her from her cha[...]
simply placed one hand under her chin and lowered his
lips to hers.

Something within Polly rebelled. He was not going to
leave her for nine weeks with only this almost brotherly
peck to remember!

When he stepped back she staggered, clutching his forearms for support. One quick glance into his shimmering
eyes. . .and she had to look away. Never could she have
imagined this fervid reaction from staid, controlled Peter!

When he spoke, she heard a vibrant undertone that
stirred her almost as effectively as his embrace. "I can
live on the memory of that kiss for nine weeks. Can you?"

JILL STENGL makes her home in North Carolina with her family. *Eagle Pilot* is her first inspirational romance novel. The setting is taken from her experiences living on a U.S. Air Force base in England where her husband had been stationed.

Eagle Pilot

Jill Stengl

Heartsong Presents

Dedicated to Dean, my husband, friend, encourager, and the best built-in resource any writer could ask for. I enjoyed learning more about your career during our "research" sessions.

Thank you to Anne Coleman and Louise Granger, two real-life MODs who gave up a lunch hour to brief me on their careers.

A special thank you to the men and women of the 494th Fighter Squadron, 1988-1995.

A note from the Author:
I love to hear from my readers! You may write to me at the following address: **Jill Stengl**
Author Relations
P.O. Box 719
Uhrichsville, OH 44683

ISBN 1-55748-928-9

EAGLE PILOT

Cover illustration by Chris Cocozza.

PRINTED IN THE U.S.A.

one

Pauline Burns stepped through a glass door into the RAF Lakenheath Officers' Club, blinking as her eyes adjusted to the indoor lighting. Pausing in the entry hall, she lifted a hand to smooth her hair. Maybe she had time to duck into the ladies' room and freshen up. . .

"Over here, Polly." Rising from the depths of an easy chair, a young officer in a khaki green flight suit folded up his newspaper.

"Oh, hello, Kevin. I didn't see you at first. Have you been waiting long?" She thrust out her hand, and a tentative smile lifted her mouth.

"Not too long." He gave her a quick survey, dark brows lifted. "Wish you wouldn't dress like Clark Kent, Babe. You're hiding your best attributes!" He bent to kiss her, but she turned to catch the salute on her cheek. "Hey, you weren't so shy the other night!"

His knowing smile rushed hot color into Polly's face. Dropping her eyes, she murmured, "But you're in uniform, Kevin," extricating her hand from his possessive grasp. "I— I've been looking forward to dinner ever since you called this morning. I'm sorry I—"

"Well, come on then. I'm starved." He headed toward the dining room, leaving her to follow at will.

Polly hurried to catch up. "You look tired. What kind of flight did you have today? Air Combat Maneuvers?"

His face darkened, "I don't want to talk about it. We've got more important things to discuss."

Most of the dining room tables were occupied, but one table near the window was available. An elderly gentleman who was just leaving the next table held Polly's chair for her, while Kevin plopped himself into a seat facing the room. She thanked the kind stranger with a grateful smile, but felt embarrassed for Kevin. What had become of his manners? "I haven't eaten here for ages," she remarked as she opened her menu, but her date only grunted. His brooding eyes roamed the room.

Polly tried again. "Have you ever eaten the halibut steak here? I'm in the mood to try something—"

He interrupted her in mid-sentence. "Wouldn't you know this place would be crowded tonight! I want to talk about—"

At that moment the waitress arrived, ready to take their orders. Kevin emitted an oath and slapped the tabletop, making the flatware jingle. Polly began to wonder if it had been a mistake to accept this dinner invitation. She was willing to make allowances, but enough was enough! She tried to make up for his rudeness by being extra polite to the waitress, but her smile felt brittle.

"Kevin, how could you be so rude?" she whispered, once they were alone. "I'm surprised she didn't toss the water pitcher right in your face! I hope she doesn't call the manager."

"Don't you start in on me," he snapped and stood up abruptly. "I'm going to get my salad."

Polly weaved between the tables after him. He muttered over his shoulder, using expletives in place of adjectives, "I'm tempted to walk out. We need privacy, and this place is a zoo."

"It must be family night," Polly speculated as a toddler ducked between them, a tea biscuit clutched in each hand. "Kevin, please remember that children might hear you. For that matter, I don't appreciate foul language, either."

"Yeah, right." Kevin scowled at the child's mother, who balanced three plates while taking salad orders from her children. In crisp, concise terms, he told the total stranger where she could go with her brats. The woman's jaw dropped as she watched him walk away.

Burning with humiliation, Polly hurried back to their table, nearly running down a schoolboy headed toward the buffet with an empty plate. She must somehow calm Kevin down and keep him from offending anyone else. It would not surprise her in the least to have the club manager request them to leave. How must that poor mother have felt when Kevin used such language to her in front of her children? Why was he being so utterly obnoxious? She bowed her head, ostensibly to give thanks for the meal, but her heart was crying out for help.

When she opened her eyes, Kevin had slumped into his chair like a rag doll, his face hidden in one hand. His shoulders sagged beneath their single silver bars. His heaped salad plate sat untouched.

Polly's heart softened. "What's wrong, Kevin? Please tell me. No one will hear us. They're all talking, too."

He picked up a fork and stabbed at his salad. "This has been a lousy week. Today was the worst." He dropped the fork, sat back, and rubbed at his cheeks and eyes, apparently ready to cry with frustration.

"What happened, Kevin?" She laid one hand on his arm, touched by his rare vulnerability.

Her compassion unloaded his grievances in a rush. "We did Air Combat Training today, and everything went wrong. My radar wouldn't work right, then my pilot went out of his altitude block and nearly collided with the other plane. I was too busy messing with my lousy radar to notice."

Pulling at his sweat-stiffened hair and biting his lower lip, Kevin swore softly. "The instructor pilot chewed us out royally. Sometimes I hate that guy's guts."

"Was he unfair, do you think?" Polly tried to overlook his swearing again, but her sympathy ebbed away. Kevin had reason to be upset, but frustration about his problems at work could not justify his disgusting language and boorish behavior. She frowned, seeing her handsome companion with new clarity.

"I don't know," he avoided the question. "The guy's a slow leak." Kevin looked up and stiffened, his eyes focused on a point across the room. He swore again, "I can't believe this. It's him."

"It's whom?" Polly followed his gaze across the room, wondering which person he could mean.

"The instructor, Pete Shackleton. He's coming this way."

The hostess was leading a customer to the vacant table beside theirs, a man of medium height with brown hair just as sweaty as Kevin's. His flight suit molded smoothly to square shoulders and trim hips. Polly didn't intend to give him more than a cursory glance, but before she could look away, he caught her watching him. Keen eyes returned her glance with an instant flare of interest.

Polly immediately turned back to stare at her salad. A little smile twitched her lips, though she wasn't sure why, and the evening took on new life. "Pass the butter, please," she asked with a lilt in her voice.

Kevin stopped staring over her shoulder at Shackleton and slid the bowl of butter toward her. "What's so funny?"

She picked up her roll and broke it open before replying, "Nothing. Am I not allowed to smile?" Kevin's lips had a selfish twist to them, she suddenly realized. Sexy and gorgeous, yes, but what a grouch he was! She finished her salad and poured more water into her glass, allowing Kevin to sulk in peace while conversations buzzed around them. The waitress brought their meals, and both began to eat silently.

A voice spoke over Polly's shoulder, "Hey, Morris, sorry about today. Things didn't go well for any of us." It was the instructor pilot, of course, standing so close behind her chair that she felt the warmth of his body. To see him, she had to tip her head back. He was smiling down at her, his eyes twinkling. "I don't believe I've met your friend."

Polly looked at Kevin, waiting for his introduction, but her date leaned back in his chair, glowering at his steak. She stood up and introduced herself. "I'm Pauline Burns, an MOD typist in the OSS building. I—I don't think I've seen you before." The pilot's nose was freckled and peeling; a bump on its bridge indicated a long-ago break. His mouth was wide and his jaw square, but the corners of his thin lips turned up, lending appeal to his tanned face. His narrow hazel eyes were framed by gold-tipped lashes.

He returned her scrutiny with equal interest. "I'm Pete Shackleton. I wonder how I've missed seeing you? I'll have to drop by the OSS more often!" His voice wasn't deep and rich like Kevin's, but it held a gentle note of humor that brought an instant response from Polly's strangely fickle heart. "Well, I'll leave you two to your meal. Pleasure to meet you, Miss Burns." He nodded and moved away.

Feeling rather guilty, Polly resumed eating, flashing a quick glance at her handsome date. If looks could kill, Kevin would be a murderer, she decided. "He seems like a nice guy to me, Kev."

"Yeah, well you haven't been on the receiving end of one of his debriefs. He's a knob. Next time, tell him to get his own date." Kevin cared not for the level of his voice. Polly was certain Shackleton must hear every word. She took a quick peek over her shoulder while Kevin concentrated on his steak and was startled to find the other man watching her. She turned back to her meal with heightened color, suddenly realizing how much she would prefer to be sitting at Peter Shackleton's table. A man with such good, respectful eyes would never embarrass a woman with crude language or behavior, she was certain.

Once his appetite was appeased, Kevin regained much of his temper and poise. "That tasted good. Thanks for putting up with me. Sorry I've been a bear tonight. It's been a rotten week." It was more apology than he usually offered. He scooted his chair closer to hers and focused his eyes upon Polly's face. "So, how was your week, Baby?"

"Fine. Busy. I helped with a party for the girls' club at church last night. That was lots of fun, but the preparations kept me hopping. Tomorrow night I'm going to a farewell dinner for Mrs. Milton—"

"Good, good." He hadn't heard one word. He began to caress her inner forearm, pushing her blazer sleeve up with one long finger. "Polly, I've missed you this week. I've been thinking a lot about last weekend."

Polly regarded her steamed cabbage with unseeing eyes. "I have, too." His touch made her uncomfortable. She folded her napkin, moving her arm out of his reach. "I think—I think we need to. . .I mean, things are moving too fast—"

"When two people are as strongly attracted to one another as we are, it's pointless to wait around. Things can't move fast enough for me! We've been dating for two months now, and nothing to show for it." He draped an arm over the back of her chair, looking down at her figure in a way that made her squirm. "Look, I know how you feel about my job, Babe, and I won't ask you to marry me 'til you're sure you can handle being a military wife, but I don't see how you could ever be sure without trying it first."

Polly looked into his black-lashed blue eyes, feeling numb. "What do you m—"

He captured her hand again. "Polly, just listen, please! Starting in two weeks, I've got a six-week deployment to Turkey. I want you to move into my place before I go. It only makes sense, with us feeling the way we do about one another. While I'm away, you'd have your chance to try out the tough side of the military wife lifestyle. It would benefit me in other ways—my house wouldn't be standing empty; and it would benefit you—no rent or utility payments, plus full use of my car. When I return, we could maybe take a Mediterranean cruise—just the two of us." That caressing voice was intended to fire her blood, but Polly's blood had congealed.

She sat up very straight, her back stiff. "Kevin Morris, I can't believe you're asking me to move in with you! You know how I feel about. . .about that. Last weekend you said we could be married right away because you were getting out of the air force." Her tight voice matched her posture.

Morris had the grace to look ashamed. "Well, that was then. . ." He gave a shrug.

"I see. It was convenient to talk of marriage when you wanted to come into my flat that night, but not now. Is that it?"

"No, no, it's not like that. You see, I *can't* quit now. I have another two years on my assignment here, and. . ." He grabbed her arm, "Polly. . .baby, if you would just give me your love for a few weeks, you'd see. We'd be so good together, so happy—"

"Love? You don't want my love; you only want—" Breaking off, she glanced around, embarrassed, and added more quietly, "If you loved me, you wouldn't ask." She jerked her arm out of his grip. "Don't touch me!"

"If you dare say I've insulted you, I'll. . .I'll—" He swore between his teeth, pointing one forefinger at her. "You're the one who keeps putting me off, saying you can't marry a pilot or Wizzo, and you hardly know me, and all that rot. I'm not asking for a one-night stand; I'm asking for a committed relationship that could someday lead to marriage. We can't keep on like this—at least, I can't. I don't want a platonic friendship with you, Babe; you've got to make this worth my while."

Her voice was low, frigidly cold. "I thought you were a Christian."

Those blue eyes flashed with the heat of afterburners. "You've got no room to talk, Miss Burns! Some Christian you are, telling people how to live their lives! I put up with your sermonizing and prudishness 'cause I thought you'd grow out of it, but you're not worth the trouble!" He called her an ugly name without bothering to lower his voice.

People at nearby tables were beginning to stare. Polly shoved back her chair. "If you feel that way about me, there is no point in continuing this relationship."

Kevin's face was crimson with rage. "That's it—I've had all of you I can take." Tossing his napkin to the table, he stalked from the room.

Polly watched him leave, her eyes wide. *He walked out on me!* She was too angry and disgusted to cry, but the lump in her chest would surely dissolve into tears eventually. Taking a deep breath, she picked up her fork and poked at her cold cabbage.

Movement brought her attention to the table behind her. That attractive pilot must be leaving. Polly wondered how much of their conversation he had overheard. Her cheeks burned; her eyes closed. *Lord, please help me get through this night!*

She heard his footsteps pause behind her chair, then move on. Her eyes popped open of their own accord and followed him across the room. He stopped at the cash register to pay for his meal, and she saw him wave a hand in her direction. The hostess glanced at Polly and nodded. Feeling more self-conscious than ever, Polly wondered, *Is he complaining about the commotion we caused? Oh, I hope not!* Not wanting to appear hurried, she picked up her handbag and rose. At the doorway, the pilot turned back for a moment and caught Polly watching him. He nodded soberly.

Polly tripped over the leg of a high chair in her path. "Oh, excuse me! I'm so sorry!" She straightened the chair, nervously smiling at its occupant, a curly-headed urchin who stared up at her with china blue eyes, his mouth outlined in spaghetti sauce. The baby's mother apologized in return, feeling sorry for the agitated young woman.

In a haze of mortification, Polly hurried on through the sea of tables. When she reached the register, the pilot was gone. She fumbled with her purse, feeling hot tears pressing behind her eyes. The hostess informed her, "Your meal is already paid for, ma'am. Captain Shackleton told me to put it on his club card."

Polly stared, one hand still clutching her wallet. "He did?"

"Yes. Lieutenant Morris's dinner, too." A simple statement, but the woman fairly bristled with curiosity.

Polly wasn't about to enlighten her. "Well, thank you, and good evening."

Walking to her car, along a flower-bordered pathway, she let the brisk evening air cool her cheeks. A pied wagtail alighted between two standard rosebushes to pick up a caterpillar. Polly stopped to watch the bright-eyed bird, and he regarded her with equal interest, but only for a moment.

With two saucy jerks of his long tail, he darted away. Polly looked after him, her eye caught by the colorful sky. It had been a balmy late-summer day, but black clouds were gathering over the western horizon, creating a spectacular sunset. Slowly she turned back toward the car park.

A two-ship of Strike Eagles roared over the base, circling toward the runway. Pausing beside her car, keys in hand, Polly watched the jets for a moment, admiring their grace and power. She was fascinated by the magnificent airplanes. Sometimes it took her breath away to think that she was involved, however slightly, with one of the greatest weapon systems in the world, and worked closely every day with the men who operated these jets. The F-15Es floated effortlessly in to land, disappearing from her field of view.

Lost in thought, she did not see the pilot seated in a car near her mini. He watched her over the top of a car magazine, sunglasses masking his eyes. After she drove away, he sat for a moment, staring into space, then folded up his magazine and started his car.

two

Polly unlocked the door of her flat and pushed it open. "Mum? Are you home?" she called softly, closing the door behind herself. It was dim and dreary inside, chilly, too. Her mother wasn't home from work yet.

Polly plugged in the teakettle and stared vacantly out the kitchen window while it heated, seeing only other brick flats and tiny squares of grass that passed for gardens. The tea sent up a heartening aroma as she poured boiling water into the cup. Feeling lonely, she headed upstairs.

In her tiny bedroom she placed the china saucer on her chest of drawers and began to prepare for bed. A spray of sea grasses arranged in a glass jar caught her eye. She plucked it from the jar, regarding it with a frown as memories of the weekend before flooded over her. Kevin, his eyes sparkling with laughter, swinging her hand back and forth as they walked along the sandy beach. Kevin snapping pictures of her with his ubiquitous camera. Kevin scooping her into his arms and running through the icy waves, thoroughly drenching his jeans and sneakers. Then, later that night. . .

"Oh, Kevin, how could you?" she spoke aloud, angry, bitterly angry. The sea grass landed in her rubbish basket.

Breathing heavily with the struggle to hold back tears, she pulled off her clothes, donned a Mickey Mouse nightshirt, washed her face, and climbed wearily into bed. Her sheets were cold and clammy. Rain beat a light tattoo on her dormer window, an occasional windy gust varying its tempo. Leaning against the headboard, she cupped her hands around the teacup and sipped slowly, thinking.

She had been tempted Saturday night, there was no use denying it. Kevin had teased her when she first refused him, brushing her lips with tantalizing kisses. When she held firm, he had swept her into his arms and kissed her with alarming passion. "Pauline," he had groaned, "don't make me wait any longer!" Pushing him away, she had escaped into the flat, her heart pounding with a combination of fear and excitement. After four days of silence, he had telephoned to ask her to dinner at the Officers' Club. He must have expected her to be frantic with fear of losing him by now, ready to fall in with his plans.

Curled up in her cold bed, hugging her legs, Polly finally allowed the tears to come. Kevin had never been her ideal man, but he was so handsome, and so flatteringly crazy about her. He had seemed to need her love, and she *longed* to be needed. Sitting up, she pounded one fist into her pillow. "With all the dozens of men I work around every day, why can't there be just one single Christian man who wants a wife? The only single men I ever meet don't care about love, and the committed Christian men are already married. It's not fair, God. It's just not fair!" Her anger drained away, leaving a hollow ache behind. "God, I feel so alone! I want just one man to love me, to really love me. . .a man I can love and respect in return!"

≈

When Polly descended the stairs in the morning, dressed for work, she found her mother seated in front of the television, a cup of tea in one hand. At forty-four, Elaine Sommers was nearly as lovely as she had ever been, small and dainty, with classic features, creamy skin like her daughter's, and abundant brown hair. She worked afternoons and most evenings at a fish and chips shop in the village, so her path and Polly's seldom crossed on weekdays. Mornings were their chance to catch up on news.

"Good morning, Pauline."

"Good morning, Mum. I never heard you come in last night."

"No, I was surprised to find you already asleep. Did you have a difficult work day?"

Checking her watch, Polly sank into a lumpy armchair. "It wasn't the work, Mum, it was Kevin. We had tea together at the Officers' Club."

"Oh?" Elaine's brows lifted. "Did you have a tiff?"

"More like a major parting of the ways." Polly had dabbed foundation on the dark circles under her eyes, but she still looked wan and wistful.

Elaine watched her daughter hop up and head for the galley kitchen. "You don't say? I thought this Kevin fellow was Mr. Right, at long last."

"Well, he's not." Polly blobbed marmalade on a cold scone and poured tea from a stoneware teapot. Peeling an orange, she talked while she ate, leaning her hips against the counter. "He wants me to move in with him and find out firsthand what military wifehood is all about. Can you believe that?"

Elaine set her empty teacup into its saucer. "And what did you say?"

"No, of course. You know how I feel about physical relationships outside of marriage, Mum. I can't understand how I could have been so blind. He's not a lonely man who needs my love. He's a spoiled, selfish liar who uses people."

Elaine's soft lips hardened into a thin line as she stared down at her fingers, clenched around the cup. "These American pilots are fascinating men. Your Kevin was certainly handsome enough to blind you to his faults."

Polly looked at her mother with mournful eyes, not bothering to explain again that Kevin was not a pilot. "I know, Mum, you warned me the first time you met Kevin." She washed her sticky fingers at the kitchen tap and rinsed her dishes.

"I wasn't going to say that, Pauline. I hardly know the man, actually." Elaine brought her teacup to the counter, her slippers scuffing over the floor.

"That, right there, should have warned me," Polly grumbled. "Had he loved me, he would have tried to know and love you, too. Well, I need to get going. Will you be going out with Wilfred tonight?" She dropped a kiss on her mother's soft cheek.

"I imagine so. What will you do?" Elaine followed her daughter to the door.

"I'm going to that farewell dinner at the Mildenhall Officers' Club. Have a good day, Mum."

⁂

Polly stowed her purse under her desk, dropped into her chair, and began to sort through her work. Catching a flash of color out of the corner of her eye, she glanced up, then looked again, her lips parting in a silent gasp. An exquisite crystal vase perched on one corner of her desk, filled with pink and white rosebuds. How could she have missed it? Propped against the vase was a small card with "Pauline Burns" written on it in bold, masculine script. *Kevin, sending an apology*, was her first thought. But Kevin's scrawl was almost illegible; this writing was like calligraphy. Of course, it might have been written by the florist. . . She picked up the card to find out. The insert bore no name, only, "P.S. With admiration, to a beautiful and virtuous woman. (Prov. 31:10)"

Polly read the inscription three times. Who could have

sent it? Logically, it must be from Kevin—but he had not admired her virtue the night before, that much was certain! She knew the Scripture verse by heart, but pulled a tattered Gideon New Testament from her purse anyway, wanting to read the words again. "Who can find a virtuous woman? for her worth is far above rubies," she read in a dramatic whisper.

The flowers kept her company throughout a busy morning, their scent wafting to her on an occasional draft. Could they be from Kevin? Perhaps he had suddenly repented and realized his error.

Just before lunch, the telephone on her desk rang. Kevin's deep voice met her ear, "Polly. . .Baby, we need to talk, and I mean now! I've got some heavy apologizing to do. I don't know what got into me last night. I'll be there to take you to lunch in ten minutes."

Polly's heart gave a wild convulsion. "Kevin, I accept your apology, but I don't. . .I'm not ready to. . .I need time to think about this."

Silence, then, "Polly, don't take too much time; I couldn't stand it! Baby, I. . .I'm in love with you!" His voice cracked.

Lips trembling, Polly struggled for words. His evident distress softened her tender heart. "Oh, Kevin, don't do this to me! I care a great deal for you, but last night. . .I mean, that shook me up. I'm just not sure we're right for each other."

He was silent for a moment, then gave a sigh that crackled over the wires. "All right, I'll give you two days, then I'll see you in church Sunday. It's not over between us, Baby. You're the only woman for me, and I know you'll come to the same conclusion. Kissing you is like. . .is like heaven on earth."

Polly closed her eyes as blood pulsated through her body, heating her smooth cheeks. "Kevin. . ." *No*, she admonished herself sternly, *show some backbone. If this is right, it will last until Sunday.* "Good-bye." Quickly she dropped the receiver into its cradle, but remained clutching it, breathing deeply.

"Lord," she whispered, grateful for the empty office. "Am I doing the right thing? Help me to know beyond any doubt whether Kevin is the right man for me! I would marry him—I could adjust to military life, I think, if only I could be sure he's the right man for me. He needs me; I know he does."

Her eyes lifted to the dainty rosebuds, and a whiff of their sweetness touched her nose. Reaching for the vase, she carefully lowered it to her lap and touched her lips to the cool flowers.

❧

Eight women lingered at their table in the corner of the RAF Mildenhall Officers' Club dining room, long after their empty plates had been carried away. It was delightful to laugh, share, and relax together, and their time was short.

Sarah Milton, the wife of a colonel, wiped her eyes, looking about at her sisters in Christ—wives of sergeants, captains, majors, and airmen—with a love that embraced each one equally. "This evening has simply flown past! I'm going to be terribly homesick for each of you!"

Two of the women needed to return home to relieve babysitters, so they all rose, still chatting happily, and headed toward the entry hall. Polly decided to visit the ladies' room, and her best friend followed. Lisa Dray was the wife of a tech sergeant and the mother of two children, but she and Polly maintained a close friendship in spite of their different circumstances in life.

As the two women straightened their hair and touched up lipstick, Lisa abruptly inquired, "So, did you break up with Kevin?"

"I'm not sure," Polly answered after an awkward pause. "Why do you ask?"

"You're not sure?" Lisa's face crinkled with disgust. "What's that supposed to mean? I want to know what's going on between you and that man, Polly. You've hardly talked to me for weeks now. I'm concerned about you; that's why I ask! Besides, I thought I saw Kevin tonight, heading for the bar with a girl on his arm. Maybe it wasn't him, but it sure looked like him."

"He had a girl with him?" Like a tape recording, Polly heard Kevin's assurance, *You're the only woman for me. . .*

"Yes, a blonde woman in a leather skirt—Polly! Polly, where are you going?"

Polly spun around, came back, grabbed Lisa's hand. "Come with me."

"What?" Lisa pulled her hand away. "I'm not rushing into a bar with you, Polly, friendship or no! That man might not even be Kevin!"

"Please, Lisa? We'll just go look, then come right out. I'm sure we'll be all right. I mean, what could anyone do in a great crowd?"

Lisa folded her arms across her plump chest. "All right, I'll go with you to lend moral support. But I sure hope Mike doesn't get mad at me!"

Polly gave her a grateful hug. "You're a true-blue pal."

They entered the bar quietly, but did not escape masculine notice for long. Two young men in flight suits accosted Polly. "Hey, pretty lady, looking for someone? You found me!" one introduced himself, blinking owlishly, but undoubtedly believing himself to be suave and irresistible.

She smiled politely, "We're looking for Kevin Morris. Do you know him?"

His flushed face fell. "No, but he's one lucky dude. Hey,

Mullens, do you know him?"

The other man looked melancholy, "Yeah, he's over there. He's already got a date though, Babe. Why don't you take me instead? I'm available!"

Polly didn't bother to respond. Lisa followed in the taller woman's wake, struggling to look confident and mature. Lisa had been married for six years and had borne two children, but she was only twenty-four, nearly a year younger than Polly, and she was very naive for a modern young woman. "Polly, must you talk to him? Couldn't we just leave, now that you know it's him?" she hissed.

As she watched Kevin smile down at the golden-haired woman clutching his elbow, Polly's expression hardened. "No, I need to face him. If I don't, I'll only have to see him again another time."

🙚

That night, Lisa snuggled into her husband's arms and related the entire story, or her disjointed version of it. Mike had some difficulty catching the sequence of events, but he knew exactly how his wife felt about bars. "Oh, it was *awful*, Mike! It was *horrible*! How can people enjoy places like that? The music was so loud, I couldn't hear myself think, and everyone was drunk. Kevin Morris was drunk, too, and he was so angry. . .I thought he was going to hit Polly for a minute there."

Allowing for Lisa's usual exaggeration, Mike responded mildly, "So, she laid into him, did she?"

"She very quietly and calmly called him a liar and a cheat and a sneak, and said she never wanted to set eyes on him again."

"That pretty much says it all."

"She was shaking like a leaf afterward, and I don't think she heard a word I said to her on the way home. That man fooled her pretty badly, Mike."

"He fools a lot of people."

"You never did like him, though, did you?"

"Never thought he was right for Polly."

"Well, you were right. She's so pretty and sweet that lots of men go after her, but not the right kind of men. She's so generous and softhearted that she overlooks major faults, or tries to ignore them. I wish she could find a man who cared enough to build a friendship with her, as you did with me. Most men look at a woman like Polly and have only one thing on their minds. Aren't there any men around who care about who a woman is on the inside? Is there no such thing as a man who knows how to give love as well as take it? Have they all died out, or are they all already married?"

Mike's shrug did little to satisfy her. "Men!" she huffed. "Well, I'm not going to give up. There must be a good man for Polly somewhere, even if only God can find him!"

three

Typing letters, writing memoranda, and putting correspondence into its proper form kept Polly's fingers and most of her brain occupied the next week. She was quieter than usual and kept to herself much of the time. The other secretaries looked at her with sympathetic eyes, but said little.

Her rosebuds had bloomed over the weekend, and they brightened her desk—and her life—with their color and scent. She still puzzled over the card, hoping now that Kevin had not been the sender. It was more interesting and romantic to imagine that some unknown admirer had sent them.

More than once she wondered about Captain Shackleton, but she had not seen him since that night in the O'Club. If he had really been interested, he could have come to see her. After all, his squadron was located right across the street from the OSS.

The roses started dropping petals Friday morning, and Polly felt a twinge of loss. Soon they would be gone, and her little mystery would be forgotten. During her afternoon break she pulled the card out, puzzling again over its message. *P.S. . . .could those be initials instead of the abbreviation for postscript? They're Peter Shackleton's initials. I wonder. . .*

It was pointless to daydream about a total stranger. Rolling another sheet of paper into her typewriter, she let her fingers fly over the keys, transcribing a letter from a lieutenant colonel to his superior.

A man in a flight suit passed the office door. That was

certainly nothing new. Men in flight suits passed in and out of that door in a constant stream every day. . .but this one was different. Though she had caught only a glimpse of him, Polly recognized him. Sitting up straighter, she felt her stomach turn a complete flip. Sure enough, a moment later he returned and walked up to her desk. "Miss Burns?"

Taking a deep breath, she lifted her eyes. "Yes? Why, Captain Shackleton, how good to see you again! How may I help you?" Her voice was ridiculously breathless.

He looked different. Tougher—older, maybe. His nose wasn't peeling anymore. He simply stared at her for a long moment before speaking, "How may you help me? I wonder."

Polly gulped convulsively, her smooth cheeks becomingly flushed. She hadn't imagined the interest in those hazel eyes; it was still there, brighter than ever.

"I've questioned almost everyone on this base about you, Miss Burns, but I finally worked up enough courage to come here and get it straight from the horse's mouth—" He stopped abruptly, an odd expression flashing across his face.

Polly smiled, her tension eased by his gaffe. "It's a good thing I like horses, or I might take exception to that comparison, sir." She watched in amusement as hot color crept upward like dye leaking from the red scarf around his neck.

"That's what I get for talking without thinking first—but if I think too much, I might lose my nerve." Placing both hands on her desk, he leaned toward her, asking bluntly, "Are you Kevin Morris's girlfriend?"

Polly blinked. "Not anymore."

"You're not promised? Going steady? No ties at all?"

She shook her head in answer to each query, restraining a smile with difficulty. "None."

"Then, if I were to ask you out, I wouldn't be poaching

on anyone's territory?"

"No, no one's."

His chest rose and fell in a great sigh as he straightened. A slow smile transformed his face with some inner quality that was quite attractive.

"In that case, may I ask you to take a drive down to Lavenham with me tomorrow afternoon, Miss Burns?"

Polly felt like squealing and jumping for joy, but she remained sedately in her chair and replied with dignity. "I would enjoy that, Captain Shackleton. I have a commitment in the morning, but I'm free during the afternoon."

"How early can you be ready?" The glow in his eyes was immensely flattering.

"Our meeting shouldn't last past eleven-thirty, and I'll be ready as soon as it's over. I can be home before noon."

His eyes scanned her face as though memorizing it for future reference. "You live in Mildenhall village, right? I live near Moulton."

Polly drew up a funny little map and tried to explain it, feeling very conscious of his fingers close to hers on the scrap of paper. His hands weren't large, but looked hard and strong. "Does it make sense?"

"I'm sure I'll find it." He checked his watch. "Wish I could stay, but I've got a crew meeting in fifteen minutes. See you tomorrow?"

Polly nodded, her smile wide and openly friendly. "At noon. And. . .thank you for the flowers?" She peeked slyly at him from beneath lowered lashes.

He stopped in the doorway, turning sideways. "You guessed!" His smile warmed her; in fact, it seemed to kindle a fire in her midsection. "You're welcome, Miss Burns!"

❧

Polly slept soundly that night, her dreams fanciful and light, full of flowers and jets. Leaping lightly out of bed at six-thirty was not her usual Saturday morning procedure, but today she could scarcely keep her feet on the floor. Butter-flies devoured most of her breakfast as soon as it hit her stomach, but she hadn't tasted a bite, anyway. She expended nervous energy by dusting, vacuuming, and straightening the small flat.

Elaine shuffled downstairs at nine o'clock. "'Mornin', luv. My, but you're ambitious this morning."

Polly gave her mother a quick hug. "I have a date, Mum! I'm going to Lavenham with a gentleman, after my planning meeting, and it's a gorgeous summer day! Who could sleep in on a day like this?" Giving herself a gleeful hug, she squeezed her eyes shut for a moment. "How was your date with Wilfred last night? Did he ask you to marry him again? When are you going to put the poor dear out of his misery and make a happy man of him?"

Though she ignored the questions, Elaine's voice was querulous. "You're so much like your father, I declare. He never grew up, either."

"What's wrong, Mum?" Polly's smile disappeared. "You didn't fight with Wilfred, did you?"

"No, dear. I only. . ." She paused, frowning, then continued, "I dreamed about your father last night. That always disturbs me." She scratched absently at the back of her neck, rattling her hair curlers.

"Did you love him terribly much, Mum?" Polly asked softly. Her mother seldom spoke of her first husband, and Polly hardly dared ask, lest the conversation end abruptly.

"Too much, I think. I should never have married John; I wasn't cut out for military life. Nothing could have pre-pared me for the shock of having my husband go off to fight in some third world country. It wasn't fair; no one could have expected me to endure it. I had no allegiance to the United States, after all." Her lips tightened and she turned blazing eyes upon Polly's face. "I don't want to talk about it!"

Watching her mother flounce into one corner of the couch and pick up the remote control, Polly felt a rush of sympathy. She only knew her father through old photographs and the reminiscences of those who had loved him, but her mother had been married to Captain John Burns, had shared life's greatest intimacies with him, only to lose him to the horrors of war. She was thankful that Elaine had not asked about her date; the less said about Captain Shackleton's occupation, the better.

Polly glanced at her watch and headed for the door. "See you later, Mum. Maybe you'll get to meet my date if you're home when he comes for me. His name is Peter Shackleton, and he's adorable!"

Polly wasn't home when Shackleton arrived at the flat. Elaine opened the door, "Mr. Shackleton? Please come in. Pauline isn't home yet, but she should arrive shortly." She stepped back, allowing him to enter. "I am Elaine Sommers, Pauline's mother."

He shook her offered hand. "It's a pleasure to meet you. Please call me Peter, or Pete." He looked about the small living room, apparently at ease, and examined a childhood photo of Polly that stood on the mantelpiece. "Your daughter looks very much like you, I think."

Elaine's smile took years from her appearance. "Why, thank you. Many people don't see the resemblance, but I've always thought she was like me. Please be seated." She nestled into her corner of the sofa, leaving him the lumpy armchair. He sat back, looking relaxed.

"Where are you from, Peter?"

"I'm a Southern California native."

"Have you been in England long?"

"Little over a year. I enjoy living here. The history in this place is incredible. I wish my family could see it. I have a younger sister who's crazy about English history."

"Do you have other sisters?"

"No other sisters, but two married brothers and two step-brothers. One brother has two children. I've never seen my niece, though. She was born since I came here." He looked regretful.

"And your parents?"

"My mother died fifteen years ago, and my father remarried. So are you from around here?" He switched the direction of questions.

"Yes, I grew up in East Anglia. Pauline was born in the hospital at Bury St. Edmunds, though she behaves more like an American. My sister-in-law raised her for many years, you see. I was unable to care for her due to illness, so she grew up in Illinois."

He nodded. "I'm sure it wasn't easy for you."

She warmed under his eyes, "No, those were very difficult years. Oh, here is Pauline. I've been enjoying your young man, Luv."

Polly stopped in the doorway and looked uncertainly at Peter, smoothing her pink print skirt with nervous hands. "That's nice, Mum. I'm so sorry I'm late!" Captain Shackleton appeared perfectly at ease, but she knew her mother's predilection for grilling her dates.

Shackleton had risen as she entered the room, his admiring eyes taking in her white eyelet camisole top and softly gathered skirt, but he only said, "No problem. I've enjoyed talking with your mother."

"I just need to run upstairs, then I'm ready. Do I need to bring anything? You have a map?"

"I think I have everything we need, but I'm never sure," he admitted with a grin. "I've been known to get lost on C-roads leading nowhere, so you'll have to navigate me there." When she returned to the living room, he held the door for her and nodded at Elaine. "It was a pleasure meeting you."

"And you, Peter dear. Have fun, children!" Elaine waved from the step, shading her eyes from the sun.

Polly glanced at him in surprise. "'Dear?' You made quite an impression!"

He smiled, gave a little shrug, and led the way to his car, and opened the door for her. "You resemble your mother, I think. She's a good-looking woman." He closed her door, walked to his side, and climbed in beside her.

"Thank you. Most people think I look more like my father. He was tall and had brown eyes and features like mine." She settled back, arranging her seat belt into a comfortable position.

Peter paused to examine her before turning the key in the ignition. "I can't imagine your features on a man. You're very feminine."

"Do you think so? I'm awfully tall, though. Five foot nine and some over."

He merely looked at her with his mouth quirked upward at the corners. His amused eyes made her feel fretful.

"Well, don't you think that's too big for a woman?"

Some of the smile left his eyes. "Does it bother you that much?"

She squirmed under his regard. "Sometimes. I don't like to feel like an Amazon."

"Do I make you feel like an Amazon?"

"No!" she protested, too quickly. "You're taller than I am, and bigger." Color began to mount into her cheeks.

"I'm five foot eleven," he informed her mildly, "One hundred eighty pounds, thirty-one years old."

"You weigh that much?" She was honestly surprised. He was trim in appearance, not stocky. "Why, I weigh—" she broke off. "Never mind."

He chuckled and started the car. "Now, you'd better get that map out and prepare to navigate."

"So I'm your Wizzo for today. Isn't that what they call Weapons System Officers?"

"You got it, but no bombs today, okay?" He slipped on his sunglasses and settled back to enjoy the drive.

"I'm not good at reading maps. I'm liable to get us lost."

He shrugged easily, shifting gears with his left hand, his right elbow resting on the open window sill as he steered. The wind tousled his straight brown hair, standing it on end. "No matter. We'll enjoy exploring wherever you take us."

Recalling Kevin's oaths when her navigational errors had once led them into a maze of rutted dirt roads between irrigated fields, Polly studied Peter's face with surprise. "Well, first we head for Bury St. Edmunds. I know that much for sure."

"R-r-r-roger." They circled the roundabout and headed toward Bury. Shackleton drove with skill and ease, keeping within the national speed limit, never giving Polly cause to cringe. She shivered, feeling chilly in spite of the summer sunshine. Her sweetheart neckline offered little wind protection, and goose pimples rose on her bare arms.

He noticed. "Want me to roll up the windows?"

"No, I'm enjoying the fresh air. I wish I had brought a jacket."

"There's a pullover behind your seat. Reach down between the seats for it." She obeyed, coming up with a chunky fisherman's knit sweater. It was wonderfully warm and smelled pleasantly masculine as she pulled it over her head. "Better?" he asked.

"Yes, thank you. Aren't you cold?" His yellow knit polo shirt revealed the well-developed muscles of his chest and arms. She caught herself staring more than once.

"No, I'm fine. So, tell me: what kind of meeting did you have this morning?"

"A planning meeting for our church's Christmas pageant. I'm helping direct it this year. It isn't a big production, but it's the first time I've done anything like this."

"You go to the same church as the Potters, right?"

"Yes. You know them? Oh, that's right, D.B. is in your squadron, isn't he. Kevin knew—" she broke off in confusion.

"Yeah, D.B.'s a good guy. I know Kevin, too, of course. How long have you known him?"

"About two months too long."

His eyebrows lifted and his lips twitched. "Don't be too hard on him. It's not easy for a single guy to live a Christian life in this environment, Miss Burns."

"So you're making excuses for him?" Sudden fear sharpened her voice.

He replied mildly, "It's not my place to excuse or condemn him. I don't know him very well, but I know enough to be pretty sure he's not your type."

She relaxed slightly. "You can say that again. Don't feel sorry for me; my heart isn't broken or anything. I just feel dumb."

"Everyone makes mistakes, Miss Burns."

"I hope this will teach me to be more careful when it comes to men. I guess I'm too trusting. It's so disillusioning when Christians don't act like Christians. Do you know what I mean?" She scrutinized his reaction.

"Yeah, I know. There have been times when I've felt like a Lone Ranger Christian—the only man around who wants to live God's way. There are other true believers around, but it's up to me to find them and fellowship with them. I couldn't help overhearing your. . .uh, talk with Morris last week, and I knew then that you were. . .well, a virtuous woman."

"You introduced yourself before you knew that."

"Well, let's say I had hopes. You. . .have a look about you. I mean, you're not only beautiful; you're a lady, and it shows."

Never before had a compliment put such a happy glow into Polly's eyes. "Thank you. And. . .please call me Polly."

"And I'm Pete." They shared a quick smile.

A tractor hauling an enormous load of carrots pulled into the road several cars ahead of them, slowing traffic to a crawl. Traffic from the other direction was steady, preventing anyone from passing.

"Guess this is gonna take longer than we'd planned on," he sighed, shifting into a lower gear.

"There's no rush," Polly reminded him. She examined his profile while he drove, wondering what he was thinking. Would she ever know this man well enough to guess his thoughts? His arm brushed against hers as he downshifted once again, feeling warm and very furry. Polly had an impulse to smooth the sun-bleached tangle of hair on his sinewy forearm, but repressed it with a little smile.

"What are you smiling about?" He cast questioning glances at her.

She decided to dodge that question. "What else do you do besides fly jets?"

He pursed his lips thoughtfully. "I like to swim, read, play computer games, take walks, lift weights, shoot skeet, play racquetball, and go driving with a pretty woman. That about covers it. How about you?"

She wrapped her arms across her breast, holding the sweater closely. "I enjoy reading, too, and I like to shop, explore historic places, hike in the woods, and do counted cross-stitch. Oh, and I help lead the girls' club at church. I don't have as many hobbies as you do. How do you find time for them all?"

"Choose what I feel like doing most and fit it into my schedule. I'm usually at loose ends on Saturdays. Of course, the pool, gym, and track on base are convenient for keeping in shape, but most of my other interests either require a companion or would certainly be more fun with one. Today my favorite hobby is driving and exploring historic places with a beautiful woman." Without giving her time to reply, he advised, "Better whip out that map. We're almost to Bury St. Edmunds."

"Oh, dear," she fretted, beginning to feel tense, "the roundabouts here always confuse me!"

Sure enough, within minutes they were traveling in the wrong direction. Peter chuckled, "Well, you warned me!" Pulling over to the curb of a side street, he claimed the map and shoved his sunglasses to the top of his head. "All we really need to do is figure out which motorway to aim for, then search for that sign at each roundabout, even if we have to circle it a dozen times before we're sure."

Polly smiled weakly, but she felt like pouting. Their first date was just beginning, and already she had displayed one of her weak points. "Things just happen so quickly in a city. I get rattled."

"Hey, I told you not to worry about it, and I meant it. I'm not angry. It's still a gorgeous summer day, and we have hours left to enjoy it. The main purpose of this outing is for us to become acquainted, right?" He gently tipped her chin up and looked into her eyes.

She lowered her lashes, feeling his fingers warm on her skin. "Right."

Before long they were on the right highway, skimming

along through the English countryside, and Polly's heart was light once more. Peter opened a new conversation, "So, tell me about yourself. Where did you grow up? How long have you been a believer?"

Polly smiled, looking down at her hands in her lap. "I grew up in Illinois with my uncle Bill and aunt Linda Weston and their three children, who are like brothers and sister to me. They are strong, committed Christians and beautiful people, and they raised me to know and love Jesus, too. After having seen Jesus in their lives, I could hardly doubt the truth about Him. They sent me to Christian schools, then to Bible college, but after my Grandma Thistle died—Mum's mother—I began to feel some responsibility toward my mother. I had come over here to visit her for a few summers while I was growing up, so she wasn't a stranger to me. She. . .she's a dear lady, but she isn't practical. I mean, she can't support herself on what she makes at the fish and chips shop, and she has no one but me to help her. So, I moved over here, went to school to train as a secretary, and took the job with the Ministry of Defense at RAF Lakenheath. How about you? What's your background?"

"Raised in a Christian home in southern Cal, second of four children. I've always wanted to fly, and my parents bent over backwards to help me—paying for some flying lessons, then simply encouraging me to work my way. I did ROTC at Long Beach State and got a flying slot in the air force. Flew F-4 Phantoms at Seymour Johnson AFB until they transitioned into Strike Eagles—that's what's called 'being at the right place at the right time.' Then I came here a year ago."

"And you've never married—" Polly could have throttled herself for that slip, but it was too late.

His eyes never left the road, but his smile widened. "Not

yet. I've been waiting for the right woman."

Polly shook her head, feeling ridiculous. She tried to joke, "You're too good to be true," but jitters gave her voice an earnest undertone.

His eyes flashed to her face. "You're not serious, are you?"

"Well, partly. You do seem too good to be true. I mean. . .I don't know you that well, but. . ."

She saw him swallow, his throat muscles working convulsively. "It's tempting to let you think I'm the supersaint type, but you'd better know the truth from the word 'go.' I'm an ordinary man, with all an ordinary man's weaknesses. Only God makes a difference in me."

"But you allow Him to do it," she remarked.

His shoulders lifted and fell. "I try to. On the whole, I know I'm living the life He's planned for me. When I look back on how He's ordered my career, I can only give Him the glory. I'm a good, capable pilot, I know, but there are many other good, capable pilots who would give their right arms to be doing what I'm doing. God put me here, and God can take me away."

Polly gave a little shudder. "I wish you wouldn't talk about being taken away. I enjoy watching the Eagles fly, but when I think about your being inside one, shooting missiles and being shot at. . ." She closed her eyes. "I'd rather not think about it. My father. . ." She stopped.

"Your father was a pilot?"

"Yes, he was an F-4 Phantom pilot, too. He was shot down over North Vietnam before I was born."

The car turned off on the road leading to Lavenham, in spite of Polly's inattention to the map. Peter spoke softly, "I'm sorry. I can understand some of the pain you must feel. I lost my mom to cancer when I was in high school. She was the best mother a guy could ask for. Losing her still hurts, and that was fifteen years ago."

Polly believed him; pain roughened his voice. "Did she ever get to see you fly?"

"Yes, I got my license before she died. But she'll never see her grandchildren or have any of the other joys of old age. My father married again and has a happy life, but it's different when I go back; doesn't feel like home anymore. My older brother, Patrick, and his family live within driving distance of the folks, but Daniel and his wife, Joy, are in Oregon. Jeanie, my little sister, married our step-brother, Vic. They live in Montana. I feel closer to those two than to any other relatives. I—" he stopped abruptly, as though afraid of saying too much, then boldly plunged ahead. "I wish they could meet you."

"I'd like to meet them, too." Polly's heart warmed.

"Hope I didn't bore you with my family tree."

"Not at all. I enjoy hearing about your family."

Silence fell between them, an easy silence this time. They drove through a picturesque English town and wound through verdant green fields. Peter remarked, "This must be the crooked mile the crooked man walked to get to his crooked house. Beautiful place, isn't it?"

"Oh, yes," Polly breathed her agreement.

"Do you feel as if England is your homeland, Polly?"

"No, not really. I love America, messed up though it is. I still thrill to 'The Star-Spangled Banner' at Retreat, and find myself singing 'My Country, 'Tis of Thee' when the loudspeaker plays 'God Save Our Gracious Queen.' There is no perfect country in this world, but I cherish my freedoms as an American citizen."

"So, you do plan to go back?"

"I don't honestly have any plans. I came here to help my mother, but sometimes I wonder if I'm more of a hindrance than a help. She might marry Wilfred—he's a good friend of hers—if she didn't have me to lean on. I had hoped to lead her to Christ, but she has no desire to be led anywhere. She feels no need for more 'religion' in her life, thank you. I adore her, I really do, but she frustrates me no end. When that woman gets an idea in her head, it's there for good!" Honesty compelled her to admit, "Of course, I'm very much like her. That's why we clash frequently, I suppose."

Suddenly clasping her hands at her breast, she leaned toward the windscreen, entirely distracted. "Oh, we're here, aren't we? What a lovely town!" Half-timbered houses and shops lined Lavenham's main street, many of them leaning drunkenly to one side or the other, some overhanging the street. A huge, gray church tower rose above the medieval buildings.

"There's the 'Little Crooked House.'" Peter nodded his head at the building as they drove past it. "We can walk back and take a closer look once we find a parking spot."

Soon they were strolling along narrow streets between the tilted buildings. Hanging flower baskets abounded in the pristine town, bringing it to life with glowing color, and other tourists strolled along the sidewalks. "What shall we do first?" Peter asked, watching Polly's enraptured expression with fond amusement. An elderly couple walked between them, and he stepped back politely, but when an entire tour group worked as a wedge to keep them separated for nearly a minute, Peter held out a hand to Polly. "I don't want to lose you in the crowds. I might never find my way home!"

She slipped her hand into his grasp, fluttering inwardly like a schoolgirl as he pulled her close to his side. "What do *you* want to do first?" Their fingers meshed perfectly.

"I don't know about you, but I'm famished," Peter stated. "I'll enjoy being a tourist more once my belly is filled."

Polly led him into a tea shop that offered a delectable selection of freshly made sandwiches, and insisted upon paying for his lunch. "It's my turn to treat, since you paid for my supper in the O'Club that night. I almost forgot to thank you—"

"Don't bother. I didn't do it out of the magnanimity—is that a word?—of my heart. It was only an underhanded means of getting you to notice me," he admitted. "I will let you buy my lunch, though, if it makes you happy."

That meal was a delight, though afterward Polly couldn't remember what she had eaten. She was more favorably impressed by Peter with each passing hour.

The afternoon flew past as they wandered through antique shops and curio shops, toured historic buildings, talked, and laughed together, thoroughly delighting in each other. While Polly browsed upstairs in a tiny gift shop with a seriously canted floor, Peter made a small purchase. She eyed his sack as they left the store, but he didn't explain.

"Guess we'd better head back soon. Want to eat dinner before we go?" He took her packages, then offered his elbow, as his hands were full.

That fluttery feeling attacked her again as she gripped his arm. "I'm not very hungry yet, but I can always eat. It seems earlier than it is."

They indulged in a light dinner in a tiny tea shop, both secretly desiring to prolong the special day. When they arrived at the car park, Peter stowed their packages in the boot of his Vauxhall. "Do you need the pullover again?" he asked, seeing Polly rub her bare arms.

"Yes, please. I'm so thankful you had it with you," Polly pulled the chunky sweater over her head and slipped into her seat.

Peter settled beside her and started the car. "Are you still cold?"

Tired and happy, Polly was feeling romantic. The idea of leaning against his shoulder was tempting. "Yes."

To her disappointment, he turned on the heater. "That should warm up soon. Better?"

"Yes, thank you." They talked most of the way home, then lapsed into a comfortable silence. Polly's eyelids became heavy. She dozed off, her head leaning against the back of the seat, her lips slightly parted. Pete found his way back without benefit of her navigational skills, pulled up in front of her flat, and switched off the ignition. Children still played on the sidewalks of the apartment complex, their tricycles roaring along the tarmac, their shouts filling the air.

Turning in his seat, Peter examined Polly in the gray evening light. Slender hands lay folded in her lap. A long brown braid dangled over one shoulder. His bulky sweater disguised her figure, but he vividly recalled her womanly shape. Her beauty aroused an ache within him.

Polly stirred, opened her eyes. "We're home!" she observed sleepily. "I'm sorry; I didn't intend to fall asleep."

Peter opened his car door. "I would likely be asleep myself, if I hadn't had to drive." He came around to open her door. "It was a nearly perfect day, if I do say so myself."

Straightening her skirt, she smiled up at him as she accepted his hand. "I would hire you as a travel agent. Thank you for today, Peter. I can't remember when I've had more fun."

His eyebrows lifted. "Honestly?"

She was surprised at his sudden sobriety. "Why, yes, honestly. I feel comfortable with you. You're great company."

He examined her face for a moment, then turned to pop open the boot and retrieve her packages. "Buy enough stuff here?"

"They're gifts for my aunt and one of my girlfriends. Birthday gifts. Want to see?" she offered, as they strolled up the walk. "You're welcome to come in for a cup of coffee or tea. Mum wouldn't mind."

"Better not this time. Thanks for the offer, though." He turned to face her at the front door, still gripping her packages in both hands. "Polly, may I see you again?" His voice was casual, but she didn't miss the tension in his body.

"Would you come to church with me tomorrow?"

The tension visibly drained away. "I'd like that. Tell me what time, and I'll be here to pick you up, unless you'd prefer to meet me there."

"If we leave here at nine, we should make it in plenty of time for Sunday school," she suggested.

"I'll be here," he promised, adding, "Perhaps we could have lunch together, if you don't have plans for the afternoon."

Her lashes lowered, concealing the satisfied gleam in her eyes. "Perhaps."

For a moment they stood facing each other in silence, then Peter spoke. "I'd unlock your door for you, but I have no free hands."

Polly immediately turned to unlock the door, then tried to take the packages from him, but he brushed past her and deposited them on the kitchen counter. Returning to the open door, he paused, "Polly, I enjoyed today more than I can say. I'm looking forward to tomorrow."

Polly extended her hand to him. "Good night, Peter, and thank you again."

No packages weighted his arms now, but he made no move to kiss her. Instead he gave her fingers a gentle squeeze, allowing his eyes to roam over her face, then lifted her hand to his cheek. "Good night, Polly."

Polly closed the door behind him and leaned against it, holding that honored hand against her own cheek. She felt slightly let down, but even more exhilarated.

four

People were filing into the gray stone church building when Peter's Vauxhall pulled into the car park. Polly felt happily conscious of their curious glances as Peter opened her car door, and even more happily conscious of his admiration. She had dressed with special care that morning, choosing a form-fitting royal blue sheath that flattered her coloring, and leaving her hair down to cascade over her shoulders in glossy brown curls. When she had opened the door that morning, his eyes had widened. "You look. . .very nice," was all he said, but Polly was satisfied. Peter looked distinguished, Polly thought, in a brown tweed sport coat and tan slacks, his cream shirt and rust print tie bringing out golden lights in his eyes.

Several men greeted Peter as they entered the building: "Good to see you here, Shack," or "Hello, sir!" from a young airman. He returned the greetings, adding his pleasant smile. Polly felt as though he knew almost as many of her church's members as she did.

Mike Dray, Lisa's husband, led the adult Sunday school class. Peter entered easily into the class discussions, earning Mike's respect with his thoughtful questions and insightful observations. After Sunday school, the two men continued their discussion of the first chapter of James in lowered voices, leaning forward to talk across Lisa's and Polly's laps. "So you're saying that all anger is sinful?" Peter asked.

"Not at all. Read verses nineteen and twenty again. James says 'Everyone should be. . .slow to speak and slow to become angry, for man's anger does not bring about the righteous life that God desires.' It's *man's* anger that's unrighteous. When you think about it honestly, what kind of things make you angry most often?"

Peter considered this for a moment, "Stupidity in other people and in myself, I guess, and injustice and misunderstandings."

"Do you find that your anger brings about God's righteous life in you?" Mike's thin face was serious.

Peter gave a mirthless sniff. "Hardly. But James expects too much, in my opinion. All my life I've been told to 'let go, and let God.' I try, but inaction is unnatural for me. I can't be good without trying, and when I do try, I usually fall on my face."

Mike shook his head, "Of course you can't be good on your own, and you can't be good without trying to be good. You need to read James again, or try Second Peter, chapter one. God's divine power has 'given us everything we need for life and godliness through our knowledge of him who called us by his own glory and goodness. Through these he has given us his very great and precious promises, so that through them you may participate in the divine nature and escape the corruption in the world caused by evil desires.' Then Peter goes on to tell us our responsibilities: pursue goodness, knowledge, self-control, etc. It's a challenge, yes, but not impossible, or God wouldn't require it of us."

Peter stared thoughtfully at Mike. "I'm sure I must've read those verses before, but I never thought about them that way."

"Say, if you want to talk about it more, why don't you and Polly come to lunch at our house today? Lisa intended to ask you, anyway."

Peter glanced at Polly, noting her hopeful expression.

"Thanks. Sounds good to me."

Polly eagerly agreed, "Oh, yes, thank you. What can we bring, Lisa? Soft drinks? Dessert?"

❧

A plastic sack weighted by a carton of ice cream dangled from Peter's left arm, and Polly claimed his right arm as they strolled up the walk in front of the Drays' home that afternoon. She almost surprised herself with this unaccustomed boldness, but something about Peter gave her confidence. Perhaps it was the way he sneaked glances at her from the corners of his eyes, or the way he reacted to her touch with a barely perceptible tightening of his muscles. It gave her a delightful sense of power. She felt beautiful, irresistible, and possessive all at once.

"Come on in," Lisa's invitation issued from the kitchen before Polly could knock. "Just stick the ice cream in the freezer, Pete. Mike and the kids are in the living room watching a cartoon tape."

Obeying this implied request to get lost, Peter left Polly to help with the meal and found Mike and the children, not watching television, but involved in a full-fledged wrestling match on the living room floor. "You look over-matched, Mike, ol' man. Want some help?"

Peter lifted a shrieking little girl into the air and tossed her gently to the couch, where she lay for a moment, laughing hysterically. A moment later, his legs were hit from behind, nearly sending him to the floor. Five-year-old Jason wasted no time on preliminaries like introductions.

"Better remove your coat and tie if you mean to help me," Mike panted. "These two are hazardous to clothing."

After untwining the little arms from his ankles, Peter tossed his coat to a chair and quickly draped his tie over it. Rolling up his sleeves, he wrung his hands with maniacal laughter, bringing screams of delight from the children. Jason and Julie swarmed over him, and he let them tackle him, careful not to crush them as he fell.

When dinner was ready, Polly and Lisa found both men pinned beneath triumphant children. Mike balanced Julie's slight body on his feet, holding her hands in one of his and tickling her under her arms. Jason sat on Peter's knees and slid repeatedly onto his belly, upon which Peter would give an exaggerated grunt of pain. Sometimes he dropped his knees before Jason could slide, calling, "Avalanche!" then tickling his small tormentor until he gasped for mercy. When the children began to call to their mother to watch, Peter scrambled to his feet, smoothing his wild hair, slightly shamefaced.

Lisa chuckled, giving Polly a sidelong glance with lifted brows, signifying her approval. "Children—all four of you—dinner is ready!" She hauled Mike to his feet, then tugged at his untucked shirt until he bent down to give her a kiss. "Darling, Peter's going to think we're raising savages!"

"Aren't we?" Mike's innocent expression made Polly laugh. Lisa's confidence in Mike's love and his evident adoration for her had often brought a pang of envy to Polly's heart. She longed to share such a relationship with a man. Today, watching Peter tuck his shirt under his belt, one lock of brown hair drooping over his forehead, she yearned to lean against him the way Lisa leaned on her Mike. What would he think of her if she tried it?

She walked across to stand close to him, unaware of the provocative glow in her eyes. Slipping her hand into his, she invited, "Come to the table?"

Instead of letting her tow him toward the dining room after Mike and Lisa, he resisted, pulling her so that she bumped against him with a little gasp. "Oh!"

He allowed her to back away, but kept hold of her hand, his eyes glinting between those thick lashes. Was he laughing at her, or did he feel the same breathless attraction that was scrambling her thoughts, filling her mind with wild imaginings? Her heart nearly stopped when he leaned toward her, but he merely whispered, "I'm only human, Polly!"

Polly brooded over this cryptic message while she ate, busying herself with cutting Julie's food and trying to not to bump arms with Peter. Color came and went in her cheeks as various possible meanings came to mind. Did he think she was too flirtatious? That collision had been his doing, not hers, but maybe her eyes had been too inviting. It was thrilling to affect him so strongly with only a glance or a touch, but perhaps that intoxicating sense of power was not a good thing. She didn't want to lose his respect by abusing her power.

The men did justice to Lisa's casserole, talking as they ate. "I'm in logistics over at RAF Mildenhall," Mike explained. "We've been stationed here, let's see, three years now. We arrived right before Desert Shield began. Lisa did most of the unpacking alone."

"I spent seven months in Saudi, but I didn't have a wife and children waiting for me back home, so it wasn't so bad."

"Yeah, but you fliers were the ones being shot at. I'm sure it wasn't all that easy. Now, what do you think about this mess in Bosnia?" Lisa interjected.

Peter shrugged. "If they send me, I'll go."

"Does it bother you, the idea of killing people?" Lisa asked, then apologized, "I'm sorry if that was an unkind question. I've always wondered about Christians fighting wars, though."

"It does bother me; I'd be lying if I said it didn't. I read a lot of Psalms during Desert Storm, between missions. David was a man of war, but he was a man after God's own heart, and so was Joshua. I don't believe fighting in wars is against God's will for me, or I wouldn't be in the military. What would've happened during World War II or the American Revolution if nobody believed in fighting for freedom? Do you believe only non-Christians should risk their lives in wars while Christians sit back and enjoy the benefits of victory?"

"Oh," Lisa sat back, a thoughtful expression on her face. "I'm not sure you're right, but I think I see what you mean."

Peter looked at Polly, but she was apparently absorbed in her meal. He continued soberly, "As the Bible says, '. . .do all to the glory of God in Christ Jesus.' If what I do is fight wars, then I must do my best and give the glory to God. Actually, it wasn't difficult to trust God during the war. The hard part is living everyday life to glorify God."

Mike nodded. "I know what you mean. My shop is bad enough, but I imagine the fighter community's even worse when it comes to ungodly talk and influences. Balancing your life between holiness and practicality isn't easy. You have to be willing to compromise on the things that don't matter, and absolutely steadfast about the things that do matter. I mean, like, never compromise a direct command of God."

"I haven't been steadfast." Peter's eyes were rueful. "I'm supposed to be an ambassador for Christ, and I can't imagine Him saying some of the things I've said. Not swearing so much, but cruel words, losing my temper about incompetence, things like that. The worldly attitudes and lack of respect for women, they've influenced me. I've kept my actions under control pretty well, but I trip over my big mouth. Jesus said our speech shows what's in our hearts, so I'm in big trouble."

"All of us fail, Pete; don't give up on yourself. Don't forget what we discussed earlier: God supplies the power, but it's our responsibility to use that power to live godly lives. We aren't robots under His control. He uses our personalities, talents, abilities, even our weaknesses, to work out His perfect plans. The weaker we are, or the weaker we realize that we are, the more we'll be willing to draw upon His power. The key to utilizing that power is knowledge of the Lord Jesus—we can't grow to be like Him until we truly know Him."

Polly was openly listening now. She watched Pete's rough-hewn profile, his firm mouth and jaw, and found it difficult to imagine him making lewd or cruel remarks. Yet he must have the same desires and temptations as other men.

"I needed to hear this today, Mike. I haven't been drawing on God's power much at all lately. I haven't been attending church or thirsting for the Word, and my life was beginning to show glaring discrepancies between what I profess and what I practice," Peter confessed. "I haven't shown God's love to many people lately. I get too involved in work, and too involved in what I want."

After dinner, the men helped clean up the dishes, then Mike asked Peter to come with him to pick up some papers at his office. Peter gave Polly a questioning glance, but she waved him on. "Lisa wants to show me some clothes she's been sewing for Julie. You go ahead." He grinned to himself as he followed Mike to his red Mazda. It wasn't difficult to guess the hot topic of conversation between those two women. His ears were already burning.

Peter enjoyed Mike's company. He hadn't realized how much he missed Christian fellowship, but something about this gentle brother in the Lord made him somehow "homesick" for Jesus. Conversation with Mike could never be trivial. The man simply did not live in a trivial world, and every conversation with him eventually came back to the central theme of his life—Jesus.

Mike was younger than Peter, but he was mature in the Lord. Tall and thin, with a pleasant, boyish face, he often gave the impression of ineptitude or immaturity, until he began to speak. He was not charismatic by nature, but he radiated God's love, joy, and peace. His willingness to listen and his genuine interest in others made him an ideal confidant.

On the way to the base, the two men discussed their jobs and spiritual difficulties, the joys and trials of fatherhood, and Peter agreed to reserve a racquetball court for Saturday morning. He felt comfortable with Mike, as though they had been friends for months.

After Mike had collected his papers and they were headed back home, he brought up a new subject. "Lisa and I are glad Polly's taken up with you, Pete."

Peter lifted one eyebrow. "Yeah?"

"Yeah. She needs someone who'll take time to build a friendship with her, and who has spiritual depth. We've been concerned about her lately—afraid she would accept less than God's best. You know she's been seeing Kevin Morris?"

Pete nodded shortly.

"Polly thought she could be an influence for good in his life. He pretended to be interested in spiritual growth, but it was all a blind, as she discovered last week."

Peter frowned. "I'm no spiritual giant, Mike. Not that I've been immoral, but my life doesn't measure up to God's standards. Yesterday, Polly gave me a gentle grilling on how I felt about Christians who don't live like Christians, and I'm not sure I measured up. It—it would be very easy for me to seek after God for the wrong reasons."

"At least you're being honest about it. She's quite a woman, isn't she?"

Pete shook his head. "That's an understatement. You know about what Morris asked her?" At Mike's nod, he continued, "I immediately determined to prove to her that I was entirely different from him, but after spending only two days with her, I'm having trouble keeping my hands to myself. He was wrong to treat her with so little respect, but I'm beginning to sympathize with him. She. . .well, she. . ."

Mike filled in the blank. "Polly's a committed Christian, but she has little common sense when it comes to men. Or maybe it's lack of experience."

"I don't mean she throws herself at me, or anything like that, but just the way she looks at me sometimes, and. . . Blast it, Mike, she's gorgeous!" He clenched his fists and stared out the window. "I can't believe I'm telling you this."

"Lisa knows her well, and she attests to Polly's innocence. We've never seen her flirt with other men. She seldom accepts dates, actually; she's very particular. I can only speak from my own experience, but Lisa behaved differently with me when we were dating than she did with other guys. She trusted me, and. . .well, she was my woman from day one. Guess that's why I married her—I didn't stand a chance of resisting! And to that confession I will add, I've never regretted marrying her. She was worth waiting for, and she's all the woman I need or want."

Peter brightened. "Polly is all the woman I need; I'm sure of that. And I know she's a lady all the way through. I'm determined to build a relationship with her on a deeper level than physical attraction."

"Lisa says Polly desperately needs someone to care about who she is on the inside."

Peter nodded. "Yeah, that's what I mean. And I'm afraid

that if I once let things get out of hand physically, I'd lose her respect and trust. She doesn't think much of fighter jocks as a breed, from what I heard her say to Morris. She undoubtedly thinks we're all amoral, self-centered jerks, so I'm doing my best to change her mind."

"I don't think that's the real reason she's set against marrying a flier. Her mother married a pilot, Polly's dad, and lost him, so she's made Polly promise never to make the same mistake. Did you notice how quiet Polly was when we discussed war today? She isn't against war per se, but she doesn't want to think about you fighting a war."

"Made her promise. . . That complicates matters." Peter's face was grim. "But if she's that set against pilots, why—" He stopped, then muttered, "She's been far from discouraging."

Mike frowned. "I don't like to suggest it, but this may be a rebound thing. For your sake I hope not. It isn't like Polly to flirt without thought for the pain she might cause. Most likely she isn't facing up to the fact that you're a pilot."

Peter muttered, "She'll have to face up to it soon." His expression bade ill for Polly Burns and her illusions.

❧

Polly glanced at Peter more than once during the evening church service, but he never met her eyes. He was apparently fully absorbed in the sermon, while Polly's attention kept wandering. Her eyes rested upon one of his hands, and she vividly remembered how it had felt to hold that warm, strong hand. She wanted to slip her hand into his, but she was too unsure of herself to try it. Ever since the men returned from their errand, Peter had been withdrawn. He had joked and laughed with the rest of them while they ate bowls of ice cream and played table games, but Polly had noticed a difference in the way he looked at her. His lips smiled, but his eyes held a brooding stillness. Self-doubts began to plague her. Was she losing his interest? What had gone wrong?

After the service, Peter hurried her out to the car. "I have work to do tonight, but I want to talk to you first," he explained as she waved good-bye to Lisa.

Polly was reminded of Kevin's constant orders and criticisms. "You officers certainly are bossy," she remarked crossly, then bit her tongue. If he was tiring of her company, snapping at him would hardly revive the romance.

Her stomach began to hurt. Instead of looking at him, she watched the passing scenery of rundown farm houses, weathered barns, and stately half-timbered houses sprinkled over acres of farmland. A pair of mallards paddled in an irrigation canal beside the road. Stately elm trees in a double line curved over the road ahead, creating a tunnel effect. The huge trees swayed and rustled in a gusty evening wind, scattering leaves upon the car as it passed beneath them. She could bear the silence no longer. "What do we need to discuss so urgently?"

"We need to discuss the future, Polly, our possible future together. That's what."

Polly's head snapped around, her lips parted. Peter's jaw jutted forward, and no smile softened his thin lips. "But Peter, we. . .we just met. . ." She gulped, immediately feeling the shallowness of that protest.

With an abruptness that rattled her still further, he pulled the car into a dirt lay-by and switched off the motor. Darkness was gathering outside, and shadows intensified the obdurate set of Peter's face. He turned in his seat, leaning one elbow on the steering wheel, the other on the seat back, and glared at her. For the first time, Polly felt a twinge of fear in his presence; not fear that he would harm her, but fear of his displeasure.

"I won't play games, Polly. This isn't a flirtation or casual romance. I want a real, lasting relationship with you, or nothing at all. Do you understand me?" She nodded, her heart in her throat. "Mike told me today that you've made a promise to your mother never to marry a military pilot. Is this true?"

Polly croaked, "Not exactly a promise, but. . ."

His retort made her cringe. "What does that mean, 'not exactly a promise?' If you won't ever consider marriage, I want to hear it from you now, before our relationship progresses any further. You can't play fast and loose with my heart, Polly! Flying is my career. I could be called upon to fight another war, and I do not plan to leave the military in the foreseeable future. I don't condone Kevin Morris's behavior, but I do sympathize with him on one point: you were trying to manipulate him into changing his career in order to win your love. Polly, when you love someone, you have to love him the way he is, not plan to change him."

He swallowed hard, his Adam's apple bobbing against the knot in his tie. "I realize I'm probably killing any feelings you may have had for me, but I insist upon honesty from the outset of any relationship." His voice was harsh, whether from anger or pain Polly could not tell.

He was right—she knew he was right—but the truth hurt terribly. Polly's chin trembled, her chest heaved with agitation, anger, and self-recrimination. She simply stared at him, her eyes filling with tears.

As she watched, the steel in his eyes softened, dissolved, disappeared entirely. His jaw worked from side to side as he struggled to control his emotions. "Polly, don't cry! I can't bear to see you cry." He rested his forehead upon his hand on the steering wheel. "I'm sorry. I had no right to be cruel. I only hoped. . ." He gulped. "I hoped for the moon, obviously. I'll take you home." He reached out to start his car.

"Peter," Polly managed, daring to touch his sleeve and stop him, "you're right. I was unfair to Kevin, and I haven't been entirely honest with you, either." Her voice had a curious tremolo, but she pressed on, "My mother doesn't want me to marry a pilot, and I. . .I guess I used that as an excuse not to marry Kevin. But when I met you, I never even thought of avoiding you because you were a pilot."

He looked up, his eyes guardedly hopeful, and she went on, "I don't know yet whether we are. . .are meant for each other, but I'd be crazy to turn you away because of your career. God could and would give me the strength and wisdom I'd need to survive as a military wife." Polly realized the truth of her words even as they emerged from her lips.

Peter sat very still, his eyes flickering as they examined her face. "You mean that, don't you? You have a right to be angry with me, Polly. I was presuming a lot and I. . .I get pretty caustic sometimes. I've been stewing all afternoon, and it spilled over onto you. I find it hard to believe that you're still willing to give me a chance, but I won't look a gift horse in the mouth."

Polly's tears brimmed, but she gave a low chuckle, pulling a tissue from her purse. "You're lucky I'm a forgiving sort. That's the second time you've called me a horse, Captain Shackleton."

"I didn't! . . . Did I?" he protested guiltily. She saw the corners of his mouth curl upward in the tender smile that was rapidly becoming dear to her. "Figures of speech can be dangerous, I'm discovering. I certainly don't think of you as a horse. Here, let me do that." He took the tissue and wiped at her eyes, careful not to smear her mascara. "I've never understood why women have to put stuff on their eyelashes. Your eyes are pretty enough already."

"How do you think of me. . .Peter?" she breathed his name, her lips only inches from his.

He sucked in a sharp breath, stuffed the tissue into his coat pocket, and began to fumble with the keys. "Too much," was his only reply. He pulled his car back onto the road, traveling a bit faster than usual, and cast a glance at her. "Are you all right now?"

"I'm not sure how I feel. Maybe. . .maybe we both need a few days apart to sort out our thoughts and feelings." She watched his profile through narrowed eyes. Just then he had acted almost afraid of her, or afraid of showing too much interest in her. Was she too obviously eager to be kissed? Maybe he was the type of man who only desired a challenge.

He circled a roundabout before speaking again. "You're probably right. I don't want you to rush into anything you'll regret later. I'm playing for keeps, Polly."

He walked her to the door of her flat, but did not come inside. "I have planning and paperwork to do tonight. Tell your mother 'hello' for me, and I'll get in touch with you. I'm night flying all this week, so won't be able to meet you for dinner, but maybe we could sneak in a lunch together. I mean, if you decide you still want to go out with me. Would you mind if I had to call you for a last-minute invitation?" He peered closely at her pale face.

"I won't mind a last-minute call, Peter. I. . ." The longing to throw herself into his arms was nearly overpowering. "I'll see you later." She quickly opened the door and escaped inside.

five

Polly didn't see Peter for several days, though she found a note from him on her desk Tuesday morning, along with a small package. He must have dropped it off after work the night before. "Dear Polly, Thank you again for the best weekend of my life. I hope you can forgive me about last night. Hope you like the cottage. I miss you and I'm doing plenty of praying. Peter"

Clutching the note in her hands, Polly tried to imagine Peter standing at her desk to write it. She had listened to the jets taking off last night with greater interest than usual, knowing that Peter was flying one of them. Already she missed him. She had given much thought to his admonition, realizing the chance he had taken and respecting him for his honesty. Instead of resenting his presumption, she was pleased by his blunt pronouncements. This man would never keep her guessing about his intentions, that much was certain, but she wished she understood his thought processes better.

Unwrapping the package, she was touched to find a ceramic replica of the crooked house in Lavenham. *So that's what he bought—and it was for me!* She held the cottage and the note against her cheeks for a moment before settling down to work. Perhaps he would call today and ask her to lunch.

He didn't. Neither did he call Wednesday. Her stomach began to ache from lurching every time her telephone rang. Finally, on Thursday, her vigil was rewarded. "Good morning, Miss Pauline Burns. Remember me?"

Polly's smile vibrated in her voice, "How could I forget, when you keep reminding me?" Her eyes lifted to the fresh bunch of flowers in her vase, carnations this time.

"That was the general idea. Hope you like flowers, because I can't think of anything else to send. Can't repeat the crooked house, and candy seems even more trite than flowers."

"I adore flowers. They aren't fattening."

He chuckled, "Like you need to worry." Polly lifted her eyebrows but let him continue in ignorance. His voice sobered. "I wanted to ask you to lunch today, but it won't happen. Things have been crazy around here this week. Can you squeeze me in tomorrow, even if I have to bring a sack lunch and eat it at your desk? I'll die of deprivation if I have to go another day without seeing you." She caught the underlying anxiety in his teasing voice. He was undoubtedly worried that she would be offended by his neglect, but she knew it was unintentional. At least, she hoped it was.

"Might we try breakfast? We could meet at the doughnut shop or Burger King before work."

He was silent for an instant, then, "It's a date." They agreed on a time and place, then he dawdled over saying goodbye. "I'll talk as long as I can. I've been scared to death—I mean, well, I hoped you wouldn't forget me this week."

Perhaps it was wrong in her, but Polly enjoyed his uncertainty. She replied indifferently, "I'm sure you've been very busy. I've heard jets flying late into the evening. What have you been doing?"

"Night TF and laser-guided bomb dropping, mostly. We all need the practise."

"What's TF?"

"Terrain-following radar. It's a radar that's built to see

the ground. It has a little computer system in it that's tied to the airplane itself and knows how fast the plane is going and how far it is from the rocks. Either we can let the plane fly itself—that's auto-TF—or use the information from the pod and fly it manually—that's manual-TF. I've been learning to do more auto-TF since I got here; we never used it during the war. The old F-111 guys here pretty much talked us into using it."

Polly smiled. "Well, now I know. I'll probably have to ask the same question another hundred times, though."

"Sorry. Just hit me if I talk too much shop. Do you have any free time Saturday? I figure I'd better stake my claim ASAP, if it's not too late already."

"I have church workday in the morning, and I promised Mum I'd help her in the garden, but maybe in the evening we could get together."

"I'm good at yard work," he hinted.

"Are you?" Polly grinned.

"Sure. Put me to work, and see how much faster it goes. For that matter, I'll join you at the church in the morning, too, unless. . .well, tell me if you're getting tired of me. Hey, sorry to cut this off, but I've got to go. Time for my brief. See you in the morning?"

"Yes, Peter. Bye!"

She stared at the telephone for a moment after hanging up, already missing the sound of his voice. He had sounded hesitant, afraid of boring her. A little smile crept over her face. He was every bit as worried about losing her interest as she was about losing his!

❧

Polly claimed a table near the front window of the doughnut shop and stared out at the puddled car park, absently stirring her coffee. Peter was late. Had he forgotten? She checked her watch again, trying not to fret. Even the thought of his forgetting their date sent a sharp pain through her heart, telling her just how fond she had already become of this man. A misty rain beaded and trickled down the window like tears down a cheek.

At last, Peter's car pulled into the parking lot. He hopped out and jogged to the shop, checking his watch with a frown. Polly smiled. His hair was wet, he hadn't shaved, and he had apparently dressed for a workout at the gym, in shorts and a flag-blazoned, "These Colors Won't Run" tee shirt. She waved at him as he approached the door, and his answering smile transformed the gray morning into a romantic setting.

He breezed in, bringing fresh morning air with him. "Sorry I'm late. I slept through my alarm." He dropped into the seat opposite, his eyes heavy-lidded and slightly blood-shot, and covered a great yawn. "Pardon me. It's the hour, not the company."

"Peter, how much sleep did you get last night?" Trying desperately to hide her joy in his presence, she spoke almost coldly.

His knees crowded hers under the small table. "Sorry." He shifted his legs, not quite meeting her eyes. "Not enough, but I'll survive. I have an afternoon flight today, so I won't be out late tonight."

"Are you hungry? I went ahead and ordered coffee."

"I brought along a banana. I'll buy some milk. Want anything? You can't live on coffee."

"A muffin, I guess." She watched him walk to the counter, surreptitiously admiring his lean legs. He looked and moved like an athlete. Polly didn't know what to make of herself. It was unlike her to notice details about a man's appearance and dress, and the thoughts that popped into her head when

Peter was near astonished her. Did he know? It was a humiliating thought!

He returned with two bran muffins and three cups of milk. "Here, you drink one of these. Women need calcium, or so my little sis always tells me. The muffins looked good, so I got one, too. Want me to ask the blessing?"

"Yes, please." Their knees touched under the table, but this time he didn't pull away. Polly put her hand on the table, and he grasped it gently as he bowed his damp head.

"Lord, thank You for this food, for the beautiful woman I'm with, and for these moments we can be together. I ask that You will bless our friendship. In Jesus' name, Amen."

Polly didn't pull her hand away, and for a long moment he stared at their clasped hands, rubbing her soft skin with his thumb. "It's been a long week, Polly."

"Yes, it has."

"I began to wonder if I'd dreamed you, yet here you are." His voice was husky.

His uncertainty caught at her heart. "I've thought about you a lot. I've missed you."

"Have you?" That boyish smile of delight finished the job. Her cold shoulder melted into a steaming puddle. She nodded, but returned her tell-tale eyes to the table.

Out of the blue, he asked, "Do you have a middle name?"

"Angela."

At her quizzical look, he explained, "I couldn't sleep last night, and got to wondering about your middle name. Angela, hmm?"

"Papa Bill, my uncle, calls me 'Angel.'" She gave his fingers a squeeze. "Peter, our muffins are getting cold, and I need to get to work."

He nodded, released her hand, and began to eat. "Polly, would you mind if I joined you for the church workday? I'd like to get involved at the church." He paused, then added, "I'll be honest, though, my main motivation for the work day is spending time with you. Does that bother you?"

She swallowed a bite of muffin, considering his question. "I don't want you to be more interested in me than in God, if that's what you mean."

"I'm not. I don't completely understand what God is teaching me, but that talk with Mike last Sunday changed my outlook. I'm not making excuses for my lack of spiritual growth anymore. God supplies the power, and I'm doing my part to live a godly life. It's an uphill battle, but this week at work has shown me what God can do when I let Him."

A smile lit Polly's face. "That's the best news I've heard in a long time, Peter."

"I have you to thank for it. Those questions you asked me last Saturday got me thinking, and Mike's counsel completed the trick. I'm back on track with God, and I plan to stay there."

He checked his watch. "What time do you need to be at work? I hope I haven't made you late."

Polly glanced at her watch and leaped to her feet. "Oh, I've got to hurry! Peter, please don't get up, thank you for the muffin and milk, and I would love to see you Saturday. The workday starts at nine o'clock. I would love to have your help in our garden, too. It sounds like fun. Don't worry about me getting tired of you—I don't believe such a thing is possible! You fly carefully today, and call me if you get lonely!"

She startled him by dropping a quick kiss upon his still-damp hair before dashing out to her car.

six

Saturday dawned gray and breezy, to Polly's disappointment. Then, to make matters worse, Peter did not show up for the workday. She struggled to hide her unhappiness from the other workers, but she couldn't help wondering why he hadn't telephoned her. As far as she knew, he was still planning to spend the day with her. Surely he would have let her know if he couldn't come.

She left the church feeling depressed. Lost in thought, she nearly stalled her mini at a roundabout, then started off with a jerk. "Stop pouting and act your age, Pauline Burns," she chided herself. "He must have had a good reason not to come. But. . .but why didn't he call me?"

The telephone rang just as she was stepping into the shower. Throwing on a robe, Polly pounced on it before the fourth ring. "Hello?"

"Polly, it's Peter. I tried to call you twice this morning, but couldn't catch you. I called the church, but no one answered. Did your mother give you my message?"

Polly struggled to sound casual. "No, she didn't. I. . .I missed you at the workday. We painted chairs for the toddler nursery and got covered in paint."

He was silent for a moment. "I'm sorry, Polly. You must have thought. . . . I telephoned last night and left a message. I had to work this morning."

"Mum slept in this morning, and I haven't spoken with her yet. She must have forgotten to write me a note. I. . .I'm glad you did call. I wondered if you had forgotten me." Her voice sounded small. "I'll miss seeing you."

"You can't get rid of me that easily. I'm about done with my work, and I've got a date with your garden, remember? Don't finish it without me, or I'll have to drag you over to fix up my place."

"Can you come for lunch? I'll fix sandwiches," Polly offered.

"Sounds great. I wasn't bold enough to invite myself. I'll be there before one, all right?"

She showered and reapplied her usual light makeup, French braided her long hair, then donned faded gardening jeans and a sweatshirt. It wasn't a glamorous outfit, but she knew Peter wouldn't mind. He was easy to be casual with, somehow. Almost like an old friend.

Lunch needed to be perfect, however. It was the first time Peter would eat her cooking, and that first impression was most important. After digging through the tiny refrigerator, she pulled out a cold chicken, stripped it to the bone, and threw together a chicken salad. Sandwiched between slices of whole wheat bread with lettuce, pickles, and tomato slices, her finished creation looked tempting. She began to slice fruit into a bowl, looking up as her mother came through the back door.

"Oh, you're home, Pauline!" Elaine said mildly. "I wondered where you were."

"The church workday, remember? I showered already, and I'm fixing lunch for all of us. Peter will be here by one o'clock, he said." Polly watched her mother's face, wondering if Elaine might have 'forgotten' Peter's message on purpose.

"Oh, he rang you up again, did he? Persistent young man," Elaine remarked. "He left a message for you that he wouldn't be coming to the workday, but I imagine you already know that. Where were you last night?"

"At Lisa's," Polly replied. "We were talking, and time flew past. How's Wilfred, Mum? Are you two getting serious?"

"He is fine, dear, and we are too old to be serious about anything. It is simply a brilliant friendship, that's all." Elaine scrubbed her soil-covered hands under the cold tap.

"Mum, you're not even forty-five yet. How can you say you're too old for love? I think that's a bunch of hogwash. Wilfred would marry you like a shot if you'd give him any encouragement." Polly scooped chopped pineapple into her bowl and started stemming the strawberries.

Smiling self-consciously, Elaine swiped a berry from the carton. "He is flatteringly ardent at times," she admitted. "But I can't imagine being married to a retired middle-school principal. He's a dear man, but he's rather stuffy."

"Then unstuff him," Polly ordered.

Her mother began to pull grapes from their stems and drop them into the crystal bowl. "It's not that simple, Pauline. You have never been married before. I have, and was mistaken twice. One must be very careful before tying one's life to that of a man, however dear he may be."

"Of course, Mum, I know that. Why else do you think I'm twenty-five and still single? Being selective is slow work. I'm beginning to believe my patience will be rewarded, though."

Elaine looked up at her daughter's face. Rosy color stained the girl's smooth cheeks, and her eyes glowed. "You thought that way about the last one."

"No, I didn't, Mum. I wondered if I might be able to be happy with Kevin. I thought perhaps I could put up with his selfish ways because he was so handsome and I thought he needed me, but I didn't long to be with him every moment the way I long to be with Peter. I feel. . .I feel complete, cherished, honored, and. . .and beautiful with Peter." Polly forgot her salad as she listed her feelings. "And I want to do nice things for him in return, like feed him a good lunch." At the thought, she went back to slicing strawberries.

"He's a pilot, isn't he?"

Polly looked down at her mother's tight lips. "Yes, Mum, he is."

"I believe you should have accepted that other fellow's offer. If you lived with a pilot for a while, you would find out what I mean. These trial periods do make sense, no matter what you say. I thought we had agreed already that pilots are not good husband material."

Polly sighed, irritated. "You agreed. I did not. I don't think a man's career determines what kind of husband he will be. Now if he were doing something immoral, like asking me to live with him, *that* would be an indication of poor character, but—"

"Pauline, I'm not speaking of character, but of the stress on a marriage caused by frequent separations, the fear of war, the fear of him crashing his jet and being killed or disabled. You don't know what it's like—"

"'Perfect love casts out fear,'" Polly quoted softly. "I don't know, Mum, maybe you're right and I couldn't handle the stress either, but I believe God would supply the strength I need. I've been thinking about this a great deal over the last few days. I believe that success in any marriage is largely a matter of commitment and determination. I'm not so naive and romantic as to think that I'll always feel starry-eyed about Peter, but I believe I would always be able to respect and honor him."

Elaine sniffed, but made no answer.

Polly enjoyed setting the table with her best china pieces and linens, finishing with a centerpiece of petunias and dahlias. A knock at the front door made her glance at her watch. It was ten minutes before one. "That must be Peter! Now, Mum, give him a chance, please! I. . .I think he's the man I'm going to marry."

Peter turned to face her as she opened the door. "Hi! I was just admiring your petunias out here. You have a green thumb, Lady." He brushed a lock of hair back from his broad forehead, then stuffed his hand into the pocket of his faded jeans.

Polly drank in the smile that lurked about the corners of his lips and crinkled his golden-brown eyes. Handsome he was not, but he was everything that appealed to Polly Burns. "Not me; Mum arranges the flower beds. She enjoys gardening. Please, come in, Peter." She gave a welcoming sweep of one arm.

He stepped into the living room, his eyes seeing only Polly. "You look ready to work. I guess we match." He wore a sweatshirt with Cambridge University printed on it, as opposed to Polly's Windsor Castle shirt.

"Very British, aren't we?" Once again, Polly had no idea how clearly her heart was revealed in her expression, but she saw the response in Peter's eyes. "It's good to have you here." The small living room seemed even smaller, filled with his vital presence.

Without thinking ahead, she slid her arms around his waist and gave him a quick hug. Suddenly embarrassed, she tried to back away, but his arms closed around her. She felt his heart beating against hers, his clean-shaven cheek against her ear, and caught the mingled scents of soap and aftershave. He was warm, solid, and. . .very lovable. Polly longed to nestle closer, to lift her lips for his kiss, but she did not dare. For a full minute they stood still, then Peter's arms tightened slightly and he spoke with a forced calm, "Polly, I could stand here like this all day long, but I don't think it'd be wise. I might die of starvation. All I've had to eat today was a bowl of cereal."

Polly stepped away as he released her, her eyes on the floor, her cheeks scarlet. "Lunch is ready." She glanced up, almost wincing, "Peter, I'm sorry. I didn't mean to be forward; I was just happy to see you. I. . .I'm generally not. . . not. . ."

His eyes were sympathetic and understanding. "I know. You don't need to apologize; I feel it, too, Polly." Taking her hand, he squeezed it gently. "Now, lead me to the feast, wench."

Peter struck up an easy conversation with Elaine, mostly relating to gardening, but she quickly directed it into more personal channels, grilling him about his family background and education. He answered with good humor, accepting her curiosity as a matter of course. "Do you live alone?" she inquired, nibbling daintily at her sandwich. Peter had already consumed two.

"Except for my cat, Wendell. He adopted me when I moved in. He must have belonged to the people who lived there before me." Peter took another helping of fruit salad. "Polly, this is the best meal I've had in months. I'd forgotten how good a woman's cooking can be."

"Thank you. I didn't exactly cook this, but I mixed it together," Polly smiled. "The chicken was left over from the fancy dinner Mum cooked for Wilfred last night."

"Those chickens did turn out rather well," Elaine beamed. "I'm not a natural cook, like Pauline, but I can braise chickens." She turned to her daughter, "Even you would have been impressed, dear. What did you have for tea last night?"

"Beef stew and tossed salad. Jason complained, but I thought it was delicious. I'm truly sorry I stayed out so late,

but we had fun talking and the time seemed to fly past."
She looked at Peter. "This is *my* turn to be sleepy."

Peter searched Polly's face, but he remained silent, trying to think of any Jasons he knew at the base. Polly noticed his serious expression, but didn't stop to imagine why
he would be upset. "Julie asked me why I didn't bring you
along, Peter. I think you've made a conquest there."

He blinked, then grinned. "Are you jealous?"

"Terribly. How can I compete with that little doll?"

The gardening was completed within two hours, the walk
scrubbed, the shrubs pruned, the grass clipped and edged,
and the small flower beds weeded and cultivated. Gardening tools in hand, Polly turned from surveying their work
to inform Peter, "Now it's time for your garden."

Elaine agreed. "Yes, I believe that would be fair. We have
hours of daylight yet. Where do you live, Peter?"

He looked from one to the other. "Are you serious?"

"Of course we are," Polly took his arm and marched him
into the flat. "Do you have all the tools we'll need, or should
we bring our own?"

"You'll probably want to bring gloves, but I have everything else. Polly, you don't have to do this," he still protested.

"I know. I want to do it, and so does Mum. She's taken a
shine to you, Peter, so make the most of it. We'd better take
two cars. I'll follow you over. Mum, do you want to ride
with Peter?"

Elaine pattered downstairs, her face glowing like a young
girl's. "I would love to, Pauline. Are you sure you wouldn't
rather?"

Polly flashed a smile at Peter. "I've had my chance at him.
Now it's your turn. Besides, you can't drive, silly!"

Elaine chuckled, "Well, yes, there is that to consider."

Peter handed the older woman into his car with all the gallantry she could desire. "I hope Wilfred doesn't see us and get jealous."

Elaine revealed perfect white teeth in a smile exactly like Polly's. "Jealous of an old woman like me? You cannot be serious." She reached over to squeeze his upper arm with dainty fingers, "My, my! I do like a big, strong man. I understand why Pauline wants to marry you, Peter. You're a prize."

Peter swallowed hard, his smile disappearing. "Did. . .did she say that, Mrs. Burns?"

She hastened to remind him, "Sommers, dear. Ms. Sommers. I married again after John's death. But you may call me Elaine. It makes me feel younger."

"If you like, Elaine." He took a quick glance at her, but she seemed to have forgotten his question.

"Do you live in Moulton?" she inquired as he took the Moulton turnoff from the A11.

"I live outside the town in an old cottage on one of the big farms. It's a nice place. I was lucky to get it." He checked his mirror to make sure Polly's beige mini followed him.

"I used to live in the country up near King's Lynn. We moved down to Freckenham when I was sixteen, and I met John at a party thrown by one of the officers at RAF Lakenheath. He was a handsome man, so tall and dark. Polly resembles him, you know. She has his wonderful brown eyes and his aquiline nose—though the nose is something of a sore point with her." She was silent for a moment, then spoke with resolution, "Peter, I may not have another chance to speak privately with you. You appear to be a good man, and I have no doubt that you would attempt to make Polly happy should she marry you, but I wish you would not ask her."

Peter had almost expected something like this. "Why not?"

"Because she needs a stable and dependable husband."

"I am very dependable, and while the air force does move people around a lot, a family can still have stability within itself. Perhaps it takes more work to keep a marriage healthy and the family strong, but it can be done, and I think Polly is capable of handling the difficulties with the Lord's help. She is not a helpless, dependent person." His voice was firm; his hands gripped the steering wheel with enough force to turn his knuckles white.

"Like I am. I suppose you're right," Elaine admitted. "She was raised by John's sister, Linda, who is a very strong woman. Perhaps she inherited some of the Burns resilience. Is this your place, Peter?"

Peter regarded the white cottage with a wry smile. "Yes, this is it. Not much to look at outside, but it's comfortable."

Polly pulled in to park behind him. Peter saw her examine his home's exterior and wondered what she thought of it. He walked around to open Elaine's door.

"Thank you, dear. You are a true gentleman." Elaine's smile lacked some of its former warmth, but she patted his arm.

"I imagine you'd like a walk-through tour," he addressed Polly with a crooked smile. "Will you let me whip through and clean up first?"

Polly chuckled. "Not a chance. This is my opportunity to see the 'real you.'"

"I do have a cleaning service come in once a week, but it's been a few days," he apologized as they entered. To his self-conscious eyes, the place looked a wreck. Dirty glasses lined the kitchen counters, and clothing was strewn across the sofa, including the flight suit he had discarded the night before.

Polly pursed her lips. "Not as bad as might be expected.

Is this furniture yours?"

"Yeah. I haven't bought much over the years, just enough to get by. Couldn't see much point in it. It's kinda bare looking in here, isn't it?" He observed his home critically. "Except for all my junk."

Polly looked around at a patched sofa, a pristine and well-equipped computer center, and a particle-board dining table with three mismatched chairs. High shelves, improvised out of planks and cement blocks, were jammed with all manner of books, from leather-bound classic novels and huge volumes of aircraft lore to paperback Bible-study guides. A weight bench under the front window apparently doubled as a coat rack for his jackets and sweatshirts. It was not difficult to pick out Peter's priorities, she mused. "Do you have a washing machine?"

"Yeah, in the kitchen. But Polly—"

"How about you start on the lawn, Mum begin on the flower beds, and I'll get to work in here," Polly cocked her head to one side, daring Peter to defy her. "I would really like to do it, Peter. It's not a sacrifice from my point of view. Would it bother you to have me clean your home? Would I be invading your privacy?"

"No. . .no, of course not. I just feel as if I'm taking advantage of you."

Elaine watched their exchange, lifting her brows in amusement. "While you two lovebirds discuss the issue, I will begin on the flower beds." She made her exit through the open front door, leaving a strained silence behind her.

A slow flush rose to Peter's brown forehead. The thought of Polly cleaning his home and washing his laundry gave him an odd feeling; odd, but not unpleasant. He relaxed, exhaling a long breath. "Polly, this may sound strange, but I feel as if I've known you for a long time."

She took a trembling breath and began to close up the cereal boxes on his table. "I know what you mean, Peter. I feel the same way, but I wonder. . ."

"What do you wonder?" He watched her bite her full lower lip and grip a wheat flakes box with both hands.

"I wonder what I don't know about you yet. Like, have you ever been engaged, or wanted to marry anyone, or been in love, and if so, why didn't you marry? I find it hard to believe that a modern man can reach thirty-one and still be . . .be. . ."

"Pure?" he supplied, leaning his hips on one corner of the computer table and crossing his arms. "I know. I had just about given up on finding a pure woman, too. We're an endangered breed, apparently. Yes, I have been in love before, a few times. I seriously considered marriage with one girl when we were in college, but it didn't work out. She wanted a career, and I wanted a career, and the two didn't mesh. I've never regretted calling that romance off. I've dated some women these last few years, but nothing serious."

"What do you want in a marriage, Peter?" She absently rearranged the boxes on the table and shoved the empty cereal bowl in little circles.

He cleared his throat and crossed his ankles. "I want the old-fashioned kind of marriage my grandparents and my parents had. I believe marriage is for life, not for romance alone, or for convenience."

"I do, too." Polly nodded, eyes demurely downcast.

"I want children, and I want my wife to stay home to raise them, to give them stability while I work to support them. I don't mean to make my wife a slave, or keep her unfulfilled, but I honestly believe that homemaking is the greatest career a woman can have. My mother loved being a mother, and I think her joy in her career showed up in how we kids turned out. None of us rebelled, we're all committed believers, and we all want the kind of home we were raised in. With my career, I'll have to be away more often than I'll like, but I believe it's possible to maintain a strong marriage in spite of separation. Trust and commitment are the keys. Like Mike and Lisa Dray, or several couples in my squadron who are content in their marriages. I also believe that romance takes work. I plan to give my wife all the appreciation and cherishing she could desire, and I won't let her forget me while I'm away."

Polly raised shy eyes to his face. "I thought you were that sort of man, Peter. I—"

A loud miaow distracted them. "Hello, Wendell," Peter bent down to pick up the enormous tabby cat that was rubbing against his ankles.

Polly came to meet the cat, letting him sniff her fingers before she began to pet him. "Nice to meet you, Wendell. You're about the biggest cat I've ever seen. And those eyes! He's very handsome, Peter. I love the markings on his face. You say he already lived here when you moved in?"

"Yup. He must have been shifting for himself for several months. The former tenants moved out of here long before I moved in. He was scrutty and thin and loaded with parasites. I coaxed him inside, fed him, and footed the veterinary bills, and I don't regret it. I'm surprised he still likes me after I had him neutered, but he's a forgiving sort. He never strays out of my garden, believe it or not."

Polly stroked the cat's black-striped back. "He's lucky to have you, Peter. You know, I wouldn't have imagined you as a cat lover."

"We always had cats and dogs about the house when I was growing up. How about you?"

"I grew up on a farm, so we had animals of every description around the place. I always wanted a dog of my own, but it never happened. Papa Bill bought me dwarf rabbits instead. I used to show them at fairs. The farm cats were mousers, not pets."

The cat's entire body vibrated with his rumbling purr. He closed amber eyes in contentment and leaned back against Peter's shoulder. Polly's fingers collided with Peter's as they rubbed the glossy fur, and he grasped her hand. There was gentleness in his eyes and voice, belying the tension of his body. "Enough about animals. I gave you my answer; now, what do you want in marriage, Polly?"

"The same things you want, and I want my husband to be a man I can trust and honor and obey with joy. A man of God."

They regarded one another over Wendell's head, almost with trepidation. Peter finally murmured huskily, "This seems too good to be true."

Then, as though emerging from a trance, he straightened and said, "Your mother is going to wonder about us if I don't get out there. Polly, you do whatever you want to in this house. All right?"

She nodded, her smile sending sparkles into her eyes, "I'll have fun, trust me! Where do you keep your cleaning supplies?"

"Over the microwave." Peter placed Wendell on the floor, whereupon the cat stretched out a rear leg and began to groom himself with great dignity. Peter pulled his sweatshirt over his head, revealing a T-shirt, silk-screened with his squadron's patch. "I was cooking in this sweatshirt. Can I take you and 'Mum' out for dinner tonight? My treat."

Polly realized that she had been staring. That weight bench was obviously not used only as a coat rack. She took the sweatshirt from him, hoping he wouldn't notice her warm cheeks. "I accept for myself, but you'll have to get Mum's answer from her. She might have other plans." Gathering an armload of his discarded clothing, she headed for the kitchen, but halted in the entryway with a little squeal. "What is that?" A small, grayish lump lay on the floor just inside the front door.

Peter came to peer over her shoulder. His low chuckle sounded close to her ear. "Looks like Wendell brought a gift to welcome you to our home." He moved past her into the kitchen.

"Is it a mouse?" Polly asked as he picked it up with a paper towel.

"No, a shrew, and a thoroughly dead one. Sorry about this. Welcome to English country living!"

seven

Peter's flying squadron reserved the first Friday evening of each month for a family night at the Panther Pub. Wives, girlfriends, and some children of the flight crews gathered at the squadron for food and conversation. Polly had gone to First Friday once with Kevin, but she had not enjoyed herself. Kevin had ignored her from the moment they arrived, and none of her friends from church had been there. Going with Peter would be different, but she still had reservations. What would people think about a woman who went to First Friday with one man in August and another man in October? It could lead to awkward situations.

For once, Peter seemed unaware of her feelings. She responded half-heartedly to his invitation to meet him at the squadron, suggesting that they eat at the Officers' Club instead, but he didn't pick up on her reluctance. "I have to fly in the afternoon, so I might be late, but you can talk with the other wives until I come in. We can go to the Drays' afterwards."

Polly liked the sound of that "other wives," and found herself agreeing to his plans. After work she went home to change and freshen up, and the party was well underway when she arrived. The pub door looked like a wall of people. Polly's stomach twisted nervously. A boom box pumped out blaring rock music; people talked and laughed above the noise. A few wives smiled at her as she made her way through the crowd looking for a relatively quiet corner, but they didn't recognize her.

"Polly?" At last, a familiar voice, a familiar face. It was Jocelyn Potter, from church. "I thought I saw you come in. Are you here with Pete Shackleton tonight?"

Polly nodded. "He said he'd be late." She tried to smile. "I feel very out of place."

"I bet you do. Here, let me introduce you around and find you a seat." Jocelyn took Polly by the arm with a reassuring smile. "I don't know some of these people, either. The turnover here is so quick, I can never keep up with new faces." Jocelyn soon had Polly conversing comfortably with two young wives who were as nervous as she was, and the time passed quickly.

Two hands gripped her shoulders, and warm breath tickled her ear. "Hello, beautiful woman. Miss me?"

Polly leaned her head back against Peter's stomach. "Not too badly. How was your flight?"

"Fine." He nodded at the other wives and introduced himself. Polly was surprised to realize that Peter didn't know everyone here, either. Greetings over, he smiled down at her. "Have you eaten yet?"

"A little. Lisa promised to have munchies for us, too, you know." She reached up to take his hand. Now that he was here, she felt secure.

"Let me get myself a plate and a soda. D. B. and Spider challenged Spike and me to a foozeball match. Want to watch?"

"Sure."

Polly enjoyed watching the game. The men were like boys, shouting and cheering over victories, muttering under their breath about defeats. Spike finally slammed the last ball into D. B. Potter's goal, shoved the markers over, and he and Peter exchanged a "high five." "Questions?" Pete demanded, spinning his players with a flourish.

Their opponents shook their heads in disgust, picked up

their drinks, and wandered away to find their wives. Peter grabbed Polly's hand, pulling her close. He seldom touched her, so this public display was startling, but she didn't mind. He must be feeling as possessive of her as she felt about him. She moved closer still, pressing slightly against him. He looked down at her, his eyes ablaze, yet questioning.

"Hey, Shack," Spike demanded. "Aren't you going to introduce me?"

"Sorry, forgetting my manners. Polly, this is George Sykes, or Spike, as we call him. Spike, this is Pauline Burns."

Polly shook hands with the big man, feeling warm under his admiring yet respectful gaze. Her cheeks grew warmer when he asked, "Haven't I seen you before?"

"I work over at OSS," she offered.

"Oh, you're an M.O.D., eh? Well, all I can say is, Pete did himself good." Spike gave her a wink, then wandered back toward the bar.

The party was still going strong, but Pete muttered, "I'm for heading out; how about you? This noise is giving me a headache."

Polly nodded, her brown eyes sparkling. Among all these men in flight suits, she thrilled at the knowledge that this man was hers, and hers alone. She let him lead the way back through the crowd near the door, clinging to his fingers.

Just as they reached the door, a colonel claimed Pete's attention. He excused himself to Polly. "I'll only be a minute. Will you be okay?"

She nodded. What else could she do? Turning back, she found herself looking directly into the eyes of a man at the bar. She immediately dropped her eyes, but it was too late. He pushed through the crowd to her side. "Say, aren't you the M.O.D. Kevin Morris was dating?"

Polly's lips parted, but she didn't know what to say. The man's name tag said "Whack Dupp." A strange name, Polly thought. He looked very young, but his eyes were bold. "I'm Polly Burns," she faltered.

He grinned, his glittering eyes sending a chill down her spine. "Yeah, that's the name. He talks about you all the time. Say, does he know you're seeing Shack while he's TDY? Not that he has much to worry about. Shack's too square to know what he's got in you." From there, his slightly slurred conversation deteriorated rapidly. He made several remarks that Polly didn't understand, then asked her a question.

"I beg your pardon?" Her heart pounded and her mouth felt dry. She didn't know what the question meant, but his manner and tone were nothing short of insulting.

At that moment, someone grabbed her arms from behind, and she was propelled bodily toward the door. "Go out to my car, Polly. Now!"

She staggered a few steps, then turned back. Peter stood nose-to-nose with the young lieutenant. His face was very red; the veins and tendons in his neck bulged. Both hands gripped the front of the lieutenant's flight suit and jerked him forward. Over the blare of music and the buzz of conversation, she heard little of his tirade, but the men closest to him heard every word. They all looked surprised, and somewhat shamefaced, while the lieutenant was utterly dumbfounded. Polly hurried out the door, then stopped in the main hallway, reluctant to go outside without Peter. She felt sick.

Peter stalked around the corner, catching her arm as he passed. "I told you to wait at my car," he ground out.

She trotted beside him, her high heels twisting as she struggled to keep her balance. "I didn't want to go outside in the dark." She gasped, "Peter, you're hurting me!"

He released her and opened the squadron door, but his fist was clenched at his side. Polly walked dazedly toward her car. "Ride with me, Polly," he ordered, then added, "Please."

She spun to face him. "Will you tell me what that was all about?"

"You don't know?"

"No, I don't have a clue what he was saying! What did he mean, Peter? And why would he talk like that to me?"

His chest heaved as he took steadying breaths, trying to keep control. "It's just as well you didn't understand."

"Peter, I want to know what made you so angry! Did I do something I shouldn't do? I don't know what happened." Her voice shook as tears threatened.

He crossed his arms over his chest, but didn't answer. Polly shivered in the autumn evening air. "Peter, please tell me!"

He turned his face away, looking out toward the runways. "I'll put it this way: Kevin Morris has a big mouth, a bigger ego, and a filthy imagination. I came this close to popping Will Landers in the mouth, but it's Morris I really want to belt." He brandished a fist in the air.

Polly digested this for a moment, her eyes widening. "Peter, what has he said about me?"

"I think you can guess." His voice was dry. "You have quite a reputation among the single guys, it appears."

"Oh, Peter, you don't believe any of that, do you?" she choked.

"No, I don't. And I made sure Will doesn't believe it anymore, either. I don't want anyone thinking things like that about you." Seeing her shiver again, he pulled off his leather flight jacket and wrapped it around her. "Still want to go to Mike and Lisa's?"

She nodded, "If you do. I could use some cheering up."

He held her shoulders with both hands, the squadron spotlights shining full on his honest face. "Polly. . ."

"Oh, Peter," she cried, and he pulled her into his arms, letting her sob on his shoulder. Another couple came out of the squadron, giving them curious glances as they passed, but Peter kept his back to them and said nothing. He was still too angry to enjoy holding Polly, but he patiently patted her back until she calmed down.

Mike and Lisa noticed Peter's preoccupation and Polly's gloom, but they wisely asked no questions. Instead of their usual Friday night table games, the couples talked quietly over cups of coffee. "So, I hear you're going to Framlingham Castle tomorrow," Lisa remarked. "We went there a long time ago. It's a good one."

Peter nodded, staring at his cup. Polly replied, "I'm looking forward to it. We've gone to a few manor houses, but this'll be our first castle. We'd better not stay long tonight. Peter had a busy week, and I'm pretty tired, myself."

Their friends nodded, and silence fell. Peter looked up at Mike, "Can we talk in private for a minute?"

The other three exchanged glances, then Mike pushed back his chair. "We'll go into the living room. Please excuse us, ladies."

"Of course." Lisa and Polly watched them leave, then stared at one another.

"What happened?" Lisa asked, her dark eyes wide.

Polly's face crumpled, but she fought back the tears. "It's nothing Peter did. He was wonderful!" Stumbling occasionally, she related the events of First Friday, wiping her eyes when a few tears escaped. "I don't know why I keep crying. I know Peter doesn't believe those nasty stories. I'm just so flabbergasted that Kevin would say things like that about me! I thought he loved me."

"Kevin doesn't understand what real love is, that's all. Peter does. I think it's exciting how he defended you! You say he grabbed the guy by his flight suit?"

"Yes, and nearly lifted him off his feet. I've never seen him like that before, Lisa. It was kind of frightening."

"I'll bet it was." Lisa chuckled impishly. "You know I adore my Mike, but he hasn't got muscles like Peter's. Whew! What a body!" she panted, fanning herself.

"Lisa!" Polly gasped, then giggled. "You're not supposed to. . .to notice things like that!"

"Why not? I've got eyes, and I'm female. Those scarlet cheeks of yours give you away, Honey—you've noticed, too. Kevin Morris is the romantic lead type, but Pete's the action hero type."

"I always did like John Wayne better than Cary Grant." The two women giggled like junior high girls.

In the other room, Mike listened to Peter's rendition of the encounter. "I don't think I've ever been angrier. I nearly punched the guy's lights out, Mike. Almost wish I had, now. I'm not sorry for anything I said. Maybe I will be later, I don't know."

Mike considered this, chin in hand. "I don't think so. You had good reason to be angry, and from what you say, I think you handled things well. You kept your anger under control, didn't swear at or injure anyone, and you set the record straight about Polly for every guy who heard you. She's not mad at you, is she?"

"No. She's only upset that Morris said rotten things about her. Do you think she still loves him?"

Mike's brows rose. "How am I supposed to answer that? Ask her, not me."

A one-sided smile twisted Peter's mouth. "I can't ask her yet. I'm not ready to hear her answer. We've been dating for going on two months now, but I still haven't told her how I feel about her. I don't think she's ready to hear it."

"When will she be ready?"

Peter slumped back in his chair, grinning sheepishly. "When she loves me back, I guess."

"You two seem to be great friends. Do you talk about important things? I mean, about the Lord and your future plans?"

"Yeah, we've discussed what each of us wants in a mate. We do Bible studies together almost every date, which helps me keep control of myself. Reminds me that God is with us. By the way, I'm learning to tap into His power, Mike. I can't say that my life is what it should be yet, but I'm on the right track. I'm enjoying getting into the Word, and my prayer life is reviving. It's still hard to find a regular time for Bible study and prayer, but I'm making an effort, and God's doing the rest."

"Praise the Lord! That's great to hear, Pete! For what it's worth, I can see a difference in you—in your eyes, your attitude."

"Thanks. I needed to hear that. I'm trying to let my light shine before men, but I'm a pretty weak lamp."

"Remember, God supplies the power for the lamp. Call it 'Operation Provide Power.'"

Peter chuckled. "I think I can remember that one. That reminds me: I'm trying to lay my worries about the future in His hands, too. You know, I'm leaving for Operation Provide Comfort in a few weeks, and Morris will be back here. I can't imagine him giving up a woman like Polly without a struggle, and he's got a legendary way with women. This'll be a faith-developing TDY for me."

"Lisa thinks Polly's smitten with you, Pete. I don't think Morris has a chance with her anymore."

Peter leaned his elbows on his knees and rubbed his temples. "I don't know what I'd do if I lost her, Mike."

"Don't borrow trouble. It doesn't do any good. We'll keep an eye on her for you while you're gone, but in the meantime, it's up to you to make sure she'll miss you."

"Gotcha." Peter stood up and stretched. "Thanks, Mike." He headed toward the dining room. "You girls ready for a game or two? Mike and I challenge."

eight

Polly dashed to the telephone, grabbing it after its seventh ring, "Hello?" She clutched a towel around herself, shivering in the early morning chill.

"Hi, sweetheart. I thought I'd missed you. Were you asleep?"

"No, I just got out of the shower, and I'm dripping all over the hall floor, but it doesn't matter."

"Sorry. I wanted to catch you before you left for work. This'll only take a minute."

"Are you flying this morning? Is something wrong, Peter?"

"Yes, I'll be taking off soon, and no, something is very right, that is, unless you've made plans for this Saturday. I have a surprise for you."

"What is it?" Curiosity mounted as she heard the excitement in his voice.

"Won't be a surprise if I tell. Don't make any plans for that morning; we'll need to be on the road early."

"I'm dying of curiosity! Can't you give me a hint?"

"Okay, we're going to London for the day. Satisfied?"

"No, but I guess it'll have to do."

"I've gotta go now, but I couldn't wait to tell you. See you tonight."

Polly passed that week in a happy haze of anticipation. Peter took her to dinner Tuesday evening and to lunch Wednesday noon, met her for Bible study group Thursday night, and Friday they had dinner with Elaine and Wilfred at a Chinese restaurant in Mildenhall, but he gave her no further clues about their big day in London. They never spoke of the First Friday disaster, but there was a new awareness, a new tenderness between them that Polly treasured.

He arrived at precisely nine o'clock Saturday morning and waited on the doorstep, shoulders hunched, collar turned up beneath a drizzling rainshower. "Great day for a drive, eh?" he remarked as Polly opened the door. Drops collected in his eyebrows and dripped from the end of his nose.

"You're going to catch pneumonia! Don't you have a hat or an umbrella?" Polly hurried out to his car, pulling her hood down around her face.

"I didn't want to drag out my 'brolly' just to run to your door. I wasn't thinking about the fact that you might not have one," he confessed before closing her door and running around to his side. He climbed in, his waterproof jacket dripping, his hair damp. "I just showered, so my hair was wet anyway, but I'd hate to have your curls get a soaking. Good thing you have a hood on your jacket. By the way, good morning." He reached over to squeeze her hand.

Polly squeezed back, then let him release his hand to shift gears. "How did your game go this morning? Don't look so surprised; my spies are everywhere."

"Lisa told you, eh?"

"Of course. Lisa says Mike's hardly ever played racquetball before. You don't beat him too badly, do you?"

"Not too badly. I play with a handicap; makes the game more exciting. He's improving fast, though; I won't be able to beat him left-handed much longer. He sure is a good guy. I'm glad you introduced us."

"Lisa also informed me that you went to the men's prayer breakfast last week. You didn't tell me."

"Slipped my mind, I guess. So, are you excited?"

"Am I? I've been looking forward to this day all week!

What are we doing first?" Polly watched the shops, the war memorial, the ancient graveyard of Mildenhall village slip past, her eyes alight with excitement. Peter circled the five-way roundabout and headed toward Newmarket. Green, rain-wet fields surrounded the highway.

"First, we drive down to Epping and catch the train. I'm not very experienced at navigating the 'tubes,' but I'm sure we'll manage. I brought along a detailed map of London," he patted a coat pocket, "and plenty of pounds for hiring a taxi, should we get hopelessly lost!"

"Oh, we'll do fine. Can you tell me yet what the surprise is?" Polly held her hands up to the car heater, willing warmth into them. Her enthusiasm for the day could not be dampened, but she might have wished for better weather.

Peter passed two huge lorries, then gave her a sneaky glance. "I'm not sure I want to tell you yet. It's more fun to keep you in suspense."

"Peter!" She gave his arm a gentle punch. "Please, please, tell me! I'll be sweet and good to you all day long if you do!"

"Hmm, that's a tempting offer, but I'm not sure you can fulfill your end of the bargain." His laughing eyes darted to her pouting face. "You're adorable when you're mad, Sweetheart."

Polly gave him an ineffectual glare, crossed her arms in a simulated huff, and turned to watch the Newmarket race tracks flash past. "I'm glad to know your true opinion of me, at any rate."

He didn't reply. Curious, she turned back to inspect his face, but found his expression unreadable. "What are you thinking?"

"I was thinking how much I love you."

Polly's pout dissolved instantly. "Oh, Peter," she breathed softly, then wasn't sure what else to say.

"I hope you don't mind my saying it. I love you more

every day."

Polly pressed her cold hands to her cheeks, feeling as though her heart would burst. The windshield wipers seemed to prompt her with their constant beat, *Love you, love you, love you*, but she couldn't bring herself to say the words. Remembering how easily she had proclaimed her love to Kevin, she wondered at herself. The love she felt for Peter was entirely different from the feelings Kevin had aroused in her, and the simple words "I love you" seemed, somehow, inadequate.

Peter glanced at her, concerned. "Am I out of line, Polly? We haven't known one another very long, but. . .I thought you knew. . . I didn't mean to make you uncomfortable. I'm not pressuring you; I know you need time to be sure of your heart."

Polly reached out to touch his sleeve. "No, Peter, you're not out of line. I just don't know what to say." There was only one thing to say to make things right, but she wasn't ready to say it. "I enjoy being with you more than with anyone else in the world."

The muscles of his jaw worked for a moment, then he gave a little shrug and sighed, "Well, that's something."

Polly pulled at his arm and claimed his hand when he let go of the wheel. "Peter, I'm not trying to let you down gently. I think I care more about you than I've ever cared about . . .about anyone, and I want to make sure it lasts." She lifted his hand to her cheek and pressed it there.

His face brightened considerably. "That's what I needed to hear." He treasured the touch of her soft cheek. "Now, want to hear the story behind this outing?"

Polly straightened, dropping his hand into her lap but not releasing it. "Yes, please!"

"Monday morning, one of the guys in our squadron found out that he was being sent early to Turkey as a replacement.

He was furious, because he had two tickets to see *Phantom of the Opera* today. Tough break, but his loss was my gain; I bought them off him on the spot! I hope you haven't seen it already?" He sounded like an anxious little boy.

"Peter! I've been *dying* to see that show! Oh, I could kiss you!" Putting words into action, she pressed a kiss into his palm. "This is better than anything I'd imagined! Is it the matinee?"

Color flooded Peter's face. He nodded. "I figure we'll have time to shop after the show and maybe have dinner. Spider told me about a great Mexican restaurant in Leicester Square."

"Spider?" Polly inquired.

"Doug Speidel. Spider. He and his wife go to the theater a lot. Knowing I'm a California boy, he figured I'd go for some Mexican food."

"I've seldom had any, if you want to know the truth. Aunt Linda used to make tacos occasionally, but that's about the extent of my experience."

The drive to Epping railway station passed quickly, and Polly was almost sorry to leave the privacy of the car for the bustle of tube stations and crowded railway cars. Few people boarded in Epping, but by the time they reached central London, the cars were packed. Peter pulled her out the door when they reached Leicester Station, and soon they were above ground again, huddled under the shelter of an overhanging roof, studying their city map.

"I think we go this way," Peter pointed left, "but I'm all turned around."

"We could ask someone where Her Majesty's Theatre is," Polly said, but he ignored that suggestion.

"We have a map and we have time before the show begins. Let's grab lunch in the square, then do some exploring."

"All right," she agreed doubtfully. "But I'd feel better if

we knew where the theater is before we eat."

An hour later, he had to agree with her. "Would you hold the umbrella for me? Thanks. I don't understand this. I'm sure we went the right way, but now we're here," he pointed to the map in disgust, "and we're supposed to be there!"

Polly had watched him become more and more exasperated, but she refrained from making suggestions as much as possible. "How long do we have before the show begins?"

He checked his watch. "Only forty minutes." Crushing the map down against his side, he gritted through his teeth, "I'm sorry, Polly. I'm making a fool of myself."

She leaned against his wet shoulder and gave his arm a squeeze, holding the umbrella over their heads. "I love you anyway, silly. You're adorable when you're mad!"

He stared at her in shock, then the sunshine of his smile burst forth. "If it took getting lost in London to hear that, I guess it was worth it!" Right there in the middle of the sidewalk he wrapped both arms around her and placed his wet cheek against hers, disregarding the businessmen and fellow tourists who ducked around them, giving curious stares and a few snide comments. After a moment, he released her, reclaimed the umbrella, and dropped a quick kiss on her forehead. "You're a good sport, kid. Your shoes must be as soaking wet as mine are. There's a tube station across the street. Let's take a train to Picadilly Circus and try from there. Wanna give it another try before admitting defeat and calling a cab?" Polly nodded happily. At the moment, not even *Phantom of the Opera* was more important than simply being with Peter.

As they emerged from the underground, Peter looked up and groaned, "This is humiliating!" He pointed, "There's the Swiss Tower in Leicester Square," he swung around and pointed the other direction, "And there's the theater, only five minutes' walk from the square. I took us in the exact opposite direction!"

"Never mind. At least we're here now. It didn't hurt us to walk."

Polly thoroughly enjoyed the show, becoming so involved that she even forgot Peter's presence for a time. During intermission, he bought ice cream bars for both of them and with an indulgent smile watched Polly leaf through her souvenir program. "So what do you think will happen?"

"I don't know. Do you? I'm afraid the Phantom will die at the end! I feel so sorry for him. I hope Christine marries Raoul, though." Her wide-eyed intensity made Peter grin, and she accused him, "You're laughing at me! Don't you like the show?"

"I like it very much, but I'm not quite as emotionally involved as you are. I'm glad you're enjoying it so much." During the second half of the show, Peter's arm rested on Polly's shoulders, where he could feel her tension during crucial moments in the plot. Once, when she gasped in horror, he gave her a little squeeze and a wink, and she smiled back, slightly embarrassed, then leaned closer to him.

When the curtain closed for the last time before the bowing actors, she turned to him with an enraptured sigh and dropped her forehead against his shoulder. "Oh, Peter, that was wonderful! So romantic, but so tragic."

"Liked it, hmm?" he mused absently, letting his fingers lightly caress the softness of her hair.

"Loved it!" she declared. "That music sent thrills up and down my spine! Oh, Peter, thank you so much for this day! I can't think when I've ever been happier!"

"The day ain't over yet, Sweetheart. Maybe we can drop into a few stores before they close for the night. I don't know about you, but I'm hungry. That meager lunch we snatched seems like days ago to my stomach." In spite of his words, he made no move to rise until she lifted her head and picked up her purse. He stayed close behind her as they filed out among the rest of the audience. Polly leaned back against him once or twice when the crowd halted, savoring his warmth and strength.

An exhausted, but blissfully happy Polly rested her head on Peter's shoulder in the nearly empty railway car as they rumbled toward Epping Station that night. She watched his reflection in the windows opposite their seats, thinking how dear he was, and how amazing it was that he had become the most important person in her world within a matter of weeks.

"Here's the end of the line, Sleepyhead." He jostled her gently. "Time to switch to the 'auto cah.'" His English accent was dreadful.

He held the umbrella over Polly as they stumbled through the dark, puddled car park. "It seems so late, Peter, but it isn't even ten o'clock yet, is it?"

"Not yet, but it'll be late by the time I get you back home, and we have church in the morning."

Once inside the car, Polly began to shiver. "I don't know why I can't take the cold. Illinois is much colder than this in the winter, but this dampness goes right through me."

"It doesn't help to have wet feet," Peter agreed wryly. "I'm sorry about that, Polly. My stubbornness wasted a lot of time and wore you out."

"Don't feel bad. On the whole, today was a smashing success. The show was fabulous, dinner was delicious, and I enjoyed being a tourist. Even the rain let up for a while! I'll never forget feeding those pigeons in Trafalgar Square— they mobbed me! But I loved it. I have fun doing anything with you, Peter, even getting lost."

At that moment, he gave a ripping sneeze, then two more in rapid succession. He pulled a sheaf of tissues from an inner coat pocket to blow his nose. Polly was horrified, "God bless you! My goodness, are you going to be ill? Do you feel well?"

Giving a quick shake of his head, he admitted, "My throat is scratchy. There was a lot of sickness in the squadron last week. I'm due, I guess. I hope you don't get it."

"Here, take off that wet jacket so you can feel the heater's warmth." She struggled out of her coat, then assisted him with his, pulling it from each arm in turn while he drove. "Do you want me to drive for a while? I will, if you like. When did you start feeling ill, Peter?"

"My throat's been kinda sore all day. It's probably just a light case. I'm well enough to drive. Please don't worry; I'll be okay after a good night's sleep. We'd better get the heater warmed up before we both freeze."

Soon they were buzzing north on the motorway, basking in the heater's warmth, listening to the soundtrack of *Phantom*. Polly rested her head on Peter's shoulder, but found it difficult to get comfortable with the emergency brake beneath her elbow. "This car was not made for sleeping," she complained, arranging her jacket over the lumpy divider.

"In my case, that's a good thing."

"True, but right now I would love a place to lie down."

In spite of her complaints, Polly was asleep long before they reached Mildenhall, slumped down so far that her head was closer to his lap than his shoulder. Peter downshifted, careful not to disturb her, stopped before her flat, and turned off the engine. Lifting her head from his arm with the other hand, he lowered it gently to rest on his thigh. A streetlight's golden glow highlighted the deluge of dark curls that flooded his lap and tangled softly about his fingers. The sleeping woman shifted uncomfortably, bringing one hand up to pillow her cheek. Peter restlessly tapped his fingers on the steering wheel, placing the other hand on the back of her seat to keep it far from temptation. In the quiet of his car with rain beating cozy music on the roof, the desire to pull her into his arms was stronger than ever before. "Polly, we're home." His voice was a caress.

She stirred, stretched with a feline grace that was nearly his undoing, opened dark, mysterious eyes, and realized that her head was in his lap. He looked down at her, his expression indiscernible in the darkness. Color infusing her face, she sat up, brushing back the cascade of curls with trembling hands. "My hair clip came out. Goodness, we're home already! I was having the strangest dreams. . . Wh-what time is it, Peter?" She searched about, finally discovering her hair clip in the folds of her coat. Her heart thumped, her breath came shallow and quick; she wondered what he could be thinking.

"Eleven fifteen." The hunger in his eyes as she reached up to restrain her abundant mane would have amazed Polly had she seen it; certainly she would more fully have comprehended the power she wielded over him. Her red cashmere sweater clung to the lush curves of her shivering figure; her sleep-softened face and wild hair somehow augmented her appeal. Shackleton threw open his car door with a spasmodic jerk and stepped into the rain.

Startled, Polly pulled on her coat and opened her door. "Peter, you forgot your coat!" He stood beside the car, hands on hips, staring into the darkness. Polly walked up behind him and swung his coat over his shoulders. "What's wrong? Did you see something out there?"

He shook his head, loosened his tense shoulders, and turned. "No, nothing. Come, you need to get out of this downpour." He walked her to the front door, but refused to enter. "I'll see you in the morning, Polly." Pressing her fingers with a wet hand, he returned to his car.

Polly wondered about his odd behavior, but her mind was too filled with marvelous, romantic memories to worry about a few moments of awkwardness.

nine

Peter was late the next morning. Worried, Polly peeked out the front door. Peter was rarely late. Could something have happened to him? He might not know about black ice. . . This was the weather for it. Thick frost rimed every car window up and down the quiet street; on the front lawn it looked almost like snow. Behind her, Elaine protested, "Close that door, Pauline! You can watch for him from the windows."

Polly shut the door, but worry lines wrinkled her forehead. "I think I'll call him, just to make sure." She had only dialed three numbers when she heard the Vauxhall's engine idling out front.

She rushed out, not waiting for his escort, and climbed into the car. "Good morning! Brr! Feels like fall today, doesn't it?"

He had started to climb out, but shut his door. "I'm sorry, Polly. I overslept." His voice was husky.

She turned to inspect his face. "You sound dreadful."

He gave one of his expressive little shrugs. "I'll live." He wiggled his nose desperately, but could not hold back a sneeze.

"God bless you! Peter, you should be in bed. Do you have a temperature?" She reached for his forehead, but he pushed her hand away impatiently.

"I don't know. It doesn't matter. I'll take you home after church and go to bed, if that'll make you happy."

"You needn't grump at me for being concerned," she

94

chided, unabashed by his gruffness. "Someone needs to watch out for you."

He gave a one-sided smile and reached for her hand. "Thanks, Sweetheart. I'm glad you care, really. I'm just mad about being sick on one of the few days I can spend with you."

"Your hand is hot and dry, Peter. Are you sure you feel well enough to sit through church? I think we're already too late for Sunday school." Polly rubbed his sturdy fingers.

"Yeah. If I fall asleep, nudge me a little."

Polly heard little of the pastor's excellent sermon that morning, and Peter heard still less. He dozed off several times during the service, and his cheeks were flushed with fever. The first few times she merely nudged him and he popped awake, but the third time he leaned heavily against her shoulder and resisted her efforts to rouse him. Polly had to poke him hard and shake his leg before he finally sat up straight, blinking groggily. Thankfully, their pew was near the back. Before the last song started, she towed him outside and bundled him into the car.

"I'll drive you home."

Without a word of protest, he slumped back in the seat. When they reached his house, he followed her inside and collapsed on the sofa, not bothering to remove his suit coat. Catching sight of a shudder that racked his frame, Polly asked, "Where do you keep blankets?"

"On my bed."

"Don't you have any spares?"

"No."

"Well, then, you need to get into bed. Come on," she took one hand and tried to haul him up, but he resisted her efforts.

"Peter, please! Now!"

"Bossy woman," he complained, but allowed her to lead him upstairs, less than half-awake.

"Now, you get undressed and into that bed, while I fix you something hot to drink. Are you hungry?" Polly felt awkward standing in his bedroom, but she tried not to show it.

He roused slightly. "No, I'm not hungry. Just want to sleep. Polly, you shouldn't be here. I'll be all right. I'd like some cold medicine, then you'd better leave."

"I'll stay until I'm sure you'll be all right," she maintained stubbornly, leaving him alone. Behind her, the bed springs squealed; he must have collapsed onto bed.

"Men!" she grumbled to herself, taking in the unwashed dishes and crumb-covered kitchen countertops. "It's a wonder he doesn't have mice taking over the place, but I guess Wendell takes care of that problem."

With a steaming cup of spiced tea and cold medicine in hand, she headed back, meeting Wendell in the living room. He cautiously circled her at a distance, then appeared to remember her, coming close enough to sniff her feet.

"Where've you been, Wendell? Sleeping? You're not much of a watch-cat. Look out now, this tea is hot." He gave a plaintive mew and followed her up the stairs, nearly tripping her in his hurry to be first at the top, then led the way proudly along the narrow hall, his tail held straight as a pool cue above his furry back. At the door of Peter's darkened room he glanced back once as if to invite her inside.

"Peter?" Polly whispered from the doorway. The room contained only a double bed with no headboard, an oak wardrobe, and a plain chest of drawers in unfinished pine. Large, framed prints of Strike Eagles adorned the walls. Grayish daylight filtered through grayish muslin drapes. He had apparently made an effort to straighten the room while she was downstairs; she suspected that most of the clutter had been shoved into the wardrobe or under the bed.

A blanket-wrapped form in the bed rolled over. "Mmmpf." He sat up, rubbing the back of his neck with one hand. Wendell hopped up on the bed and rubbed his head against Peter's side, purring noisily, then hooked a paw into a gaping hole in the front of his master's T-shirt and rolled over, playfully biting and kicking at the tattered fabric. Peter shoved him away. "Knock it off, Wendell." The cat gave his hand a nip before leaping from the bed and galloping down the hallway.

"Did he put those holes in your shirt?" Polly asked, amused. The faded Grand Canyon T-shirt looked long overdue for the ragbag. "Don't you have any better nightshirts than that?"

"It's comfortable. He just enlarges the holes. I'm his favorite chew toy."

"You sound awful, Peter. Is it mostly your throat that hurts?"

"Yeah. My head aches, too."

She sat on the edge of his bed, wondering if his sheets had been washed since the day she cleaned his house. "Here's your tea and some cold medicine. I don't know if it'll help, but it's worth a try."

He nodded meekly and accepted the tablets. She watched him swallow them with a cautious sip of the tea. "I should have brought you some water, too. I wish you had a thermometer. Mama Lin, my aunt, says men are lousy patients. They either suffer in martyrlike silence, or they demand to be coddled. Either way, they're grouchy as bears. Which sort are you?"

He glared at her over his teacup.

"You look dangerous, but you're too sick to frighten me. Finish that tea, then I'll let you sleep. No, come to think of it. . . Have you changed these sheets since I cleaned your house that day?"

His guilty expression was her answer.

"I didn't think so. Now, you wrap up in that blanket and sit over here while I change your bed. There's nothing worse than sleeping in a dirty bed, especially when you're sick."

He obeyed without a murmur, clutching the blanket around his shoulders while he watched her work. When she had finished, he sank back against his plumped pillows with a rather pitiful sigh. Polly smiled, thinking that he must be the martyr type.

"Thank you, Polly," he half-whispered. "It does feel better."

She hovered at his bedside for another moment. "Are you sure I can't do anything else for you? Do you want some soup? There's a can of chicken with stars in your pantry." He only shook his head. "All right. I'll be downstairs cleaning if you need me." There was no reply. His breathing was already deep and hoarse. Polly could almost see the Zs forming over his head. She stroked his smooth, hot cheek one last time, then tiptoed from the room.

&

Mike and Lisa invited her home for soup after the evening church service. Polly was impressed by the way Mike offered to put the children to bed, leaving the women to talk. "What a sweetheart!" she remarked to Lisa. "How did you train that man?"

Lisa chuckled. "I didn't do a thing. His mother gets all the credit. He's especially thoughtful when I'm pregnant."

It took a moment, but Polly caught the hint. "Lisa, are you expecting?" The other woman's smile was sufficient reply. "Oh, Lis, I'm so happy for you! When are you due?"

"Not 'til May, but I usually deliver early."

"So, Jason and Julie will be big brother and sister. Have you told them yet?"

"Not yet. I only found out for sure the other day, although I've suspected for a few weeks now."

Polly wasn't aware that her wistful face revealed her thoughts. "So, when are you going to settle down and have a family, Pollywog?"

"Soon, I hope. I don't know, though; Peter wasn't himself today. I hope he isn't getting tired of me." She dipped a cracker into her soup, then forgot to eat it.

"Do you care about much of anything when you're sick?" Lisa asked. "Don't get down on him for that, Polly. You have a few weeks left with him before he leaves, at least."

Polly's face fell even further. "Yeah, three more weeks before he goes to Turkey. I can't imagine what it'll be like to have him gone for six whole weeks, Lisa! I hardly survived church this evening. I guess this separation will be the acid test of my endurance, and of our love. What if he forgets me while he's away?"

"Not likely. By the way, has Kevin ever tried to contact you since our 'barroom brawl'?"

"He telephoned a few days later to apologize, but I wasn't in much of a mood to talk." Polly's voice held distaste. "He's in Turkey now."

"What if Kevin were to straighten out and get his life right with God?"

Polly looked startled. "That's highly unlikely. Kevin has no interest in surrendering his life to Christ."

Lisa gave a little sigh, her lips pursed. "I don't know, Polly. Sometimes I think you still care more for Kevin than you'll admit."

Polly flushed. "Nonsense. I lost any remaining illusions

about Kevin at First Friday. I only. . ."

"You only what?"

"My only complaint with Peter is that he never kisses me. That sounds silly, doesn't it? But how would you feel if Mike never wanted to kiss you?"

"Pete wants to kiss you, Pauline Burns; anyone can see that. He has more self-control than most men do, and I think he loves you more than most men could. He knows what Kevin demanded from you, and he wants you to know beyond any doubt that his love for you is different. His isn't a demanding love, but a giving love. Can't you see that?"

Polly stared at the table, her thoughts whirling. "I think I see what you mean, Lisa. I'm being silly and insecure, I guess. I know he's attracted to me, but I just wish his attraction was stronger than his self-control at least some of the time. At least enough for one kiss!"

Lisa laced her fingers and placed them on top of her head. "Think about it, Polly: if he has self-control enough to wait this long to kiss you, you'll never have to worry about him being unfaithful, even when he's on a long TDY. He's proven his strength of character beyond a doubt."

Polly considered this for a few moments, then nodded. "You're absolutely right, Lisa. In my more lucid moments, I value his high morals. God must have known that I needed a man like him. I want so much to be desired and needed that I forget how important other aspects of our relationship are."

"Just enjoy your dear man while you have him here. He really is a sweetheart, Polly, and I wouldn't worry about his being immune to you. Mike doesn't betray much of what Peter confides in him, but he's let enough slip to assure me that Pete's a normal man."

ten

Reality, USAF style, hit Polly with a vengeance Monday morning. At nine o'clock she was typing busily, thinking that during her break she would ring Peter and get an update on his condition. Her telephone rang. "Current Ops, Polly speaking."

Peter didn't bother to introduce himself, though his voice was a mere croak. "Polly, have you heard about Captain Halberd?"

"No, what's wrong, Peter? Where are you?"

"Brian Halberd is going to SOS in Alabama—they're recalling him from Operation Provide Comfort immediately, and I'm the only one qualified to replace him. I'm at the squadron right now, but I'll be flying out late this afternoon on a 135 from RAF Mildenhall. I barely have time to outprocess and get home to pack."

"Oh." It came out as a strained squeak. "But, Peter, you're sick. . ."

"Once I'm on that plane, I can sit back and relax. I'll recover in Turkey. Sweetheart, I'll try to stop in and say goodbye, but it won't be much—no privacy, and I won't be back until mid-December. Polly—" Other men talked and laughed in the background, making it difficult to hear his hoarse voice. "Polly, I love you. Don't give up on me, please! We'll be the same when I get back?"

His almost frantic plea choked her up even more. "Yes, Peter. I'll be waiting," she managed, then felt more confident. Yes, she would wait for him, if it took six months, a year, five years. "I love you, too, Peter."

She worked straight through her lunch break that day, for she needed to concentrate on something other than the aching emptiness in her heart. Finally, she crossed her arms and dropped her head into them. *Lord*, it was an inward groan, *Help me! You promised strength when I need it, and I need it now! If I am to marry Peter, I must adjust to these separations and learn not to resent them or him. It is part of his career, therefore it's a part of him which I must learn to accept, and accept with grace. I don't want to tell him goodbye today as though I'll never see him again—that would hurt him terribly. I must be brave and loving and cheerful, but still let him know how much I'll miss him.*

Sitting up, she wiped her eyes with a tissue and continued, *Thank You for this chance to prepare myself. I don't want to create a scene or embarrass him, and it would be equally bad to act cold and unconcerned.* Squaring her shoulders, she decided, *December isn't that far off, after all.*

Peter did not show up until nearly three o'clock. His face showed the strain he was under, emotionally and physically. Polly jumped up as he entered the office, begging, "Peter, please sit down. You look ready to drop!" She glanced around, but Vicky was not at her desk, and the other officers couldn't see into her cubicle from their desks. It wasn't exactly private, but she would make the best of the situation.

He blinked, having halfway expected her to sob and berate him for leaving her, and obediently sank into a chair across from her desk. "Thank you. You're right, I'm dead on my feet. Before I forget, I have a favor to ask you. Would you feed Wendell while I'm away? I don't have time to ask my neighbors. I know it's an inconven—"

"Of course, I'll be happy to do it! If you like, I could move into your cottage while you're away and keep up with your bills and such." The thought had only just popped into her head, but it seemed logical.

He considered. "I'm not sure it would look good. People might think. . .well, you know."

"I'll tell everyone that it's only for while you're gone. Please, let me do this for you, Peter. It'll make things easier for me, in a way. I'll feel more tied to you."

His eyes widened. "That's a tempting thought." He worried his flight cap between his fingers and finally shook his head. "Maybe you could stay there overnight once or twice to keep Wendell company, but I don't think you ought to actually move in, Polly. It just doesn't look right."

Polly sighed, but gave in gracefully. "Very well. I can still keep up your bills for you, though. I'm sure you haven't had time to arrange that sort of thing."

"I don't think you'll need to—most of them are directly debited from my account—but you could bring in my mail. Here's my house key; I have a spare hidden in the shed. I'll leave the keys to the car in the house. You can drive it, or just start it up occasionally. I'll be taking a taxi to the airfield." He informed her about Wendell's care and feeding, then checked his watch and ran his fingers through his short hair in frustration. "This is a terrible way to say good-bye, Polly. I wish. . .but it doesn't do any good to wish." His eyes focused on her lips with an expression Polly had never seen in them before.

Her heart lurched, then began to beat double-time. "Are you allowed to kiss me good-bye?" she asked softly. "Just one little kiss?"

The despairing look in his eyes lightened. "Yes, I think so, under the circumstances." He glanced around. "This isn't the setting I'd planned for our first kiss, but it'll have to do."

Circling the desk, he pulled her from her chair, his eyes still focused on her lips, their heavy lashes concealing his thoughts. Did he despise her for begging his kiss? She felt awkward and vulnerable, and her feelings must have shown, for he simply placed one hand under her chin and lowered his chapped lips to hers.

Something within Polly rebelled. He was not going to leave her for nine weeks with only this almost brotherly peck to remember! Before their lips could part, she slid her hands over the velcroed name tag and zippered pockets on his chest, and pressed her fingers against the back of his neck, leaning brazenly against him. The desired response came with reassuring speed—immediately his arms crushed her to his chest and his lips demanded all the love she could give. Polly held nothing back, longing only to be closer to him.

When he stepped back she staggered, clutching his forearms for support. One quick glance into his shimmering eyes. . .and she had to look away. Never could she have imagined this fervid reaction from staid, controlled Peter!

When he spoke, she heard a vibrant undertone that stirred her almost as effectively as his embrace. "I can live on the memory of that kiss for nine weeks. Can you?"

Polly wasn't conscious of the invitation in her eyes. "I'll have another one waiting for you when you return, Peter."

He drew a sharp breath and began to reach for her, but at that moment Vicky stepped through the doorway and returned to her desk, giving them a wicked little smile. "Is it safe to come in yet?"

Polly flushed. Vicky must have witnessed their kiss. "Captain Shackleton is leaving for Incirlik today," she explained weakly.

"You could walk him to the front door, Polly. No one will mind."

Polly took her advice, strolling beside Peter along the hallway between framed photographs of air force jets, past and present. Other busy officers passed down the hallway, greeting them both by name. The lovers spoke in calm, level voices, conscious of possible listening ears, but whenever their eyes met, silent messages passed between them like lightning bolts. For the first time in her acquaintance with Peter, Polly found herself flustered by the messages in his eyes. He kept them circumspectly on her face, as he almost always did, but she knew exactly what he was thinking. And she had doubted her ability to stir his senses!

In the entryway he turned abruptly to face her. "I haven't dared to ask you this before, but. . .will you promise not to see other men while I'm away? I'll be blunt, Polly: I couldn't bear to think of you kissing another man like that." His neck matched his red scarf in hue, and the color crept up to his cheekbones. "I haven't so much as noticed another woman since the day I first laid eyes on you, but I can't expect you to feel the same way about me. I'm not much to look at."

Polly longed to touch the fanned lines at the outer corners of his eyes, to smooth his hair, to frame the planes of his face with her hands and engrave them upon her heart for future reference, but she knew she could not. Public display of affection would be highly inappropriate, and might get him into trouble. Color tinged her pale cheeks, "You're the only man I care to look at, Peter, and. . . I've never kissed any man the way I just kissed you. I promise I'll stick to Lisa and Jocelyn and my other girl-type friends for the next nine weeks. I trust you'll be true to me, too."

"I will. I wish I had a photograph of you, Polly. Come to think of it, I do have a roll of film from our day in London. I'll get it developed in Turkey. That's something to look forward to."

He glanced through the glass doors at the driving rain. "Well, I've got to go." He gave her hand one last squeeze. "I'll pray for you every day, Polly, my. . .my dear; I always do. Until December, then. We'll have a Christmas like no other!"

"Have a good trip, Peter, and get well soon. I'll be praying for you, too. 'Bye!" She smiled brightly until he disappeared from view, though tears smarted in her eyes.

Vicky greeted her with that same knowing grin when she returned to her desk. "Now that was what I call a good-bye kiss! Do you give every departing pilot a kiss like that? Didn't know the stern Captain Shackleton had it in him! Whew! This room is still sizzling! What will Kevin have to say about this when he returns? I wonder."

Polly only gave her a wistful smile in return. Vicky never would believe that she preferred Peter to Kevin. It wasn't worth arguing about.

eleven

Black clouds hemmed the air base on every side, portending storms to come, but right over RAF Mildenhall the sky was clear, showing a few early stars. Polly huddled inside her mini, unwilling to brave the icy wind that buffeted her car. Other "bird-watchers" more intrepid than herself trained their binoculars on the gray tanker taxiing slowly beside the runway. The Ministry of Defense had designated this little car park for those who made a hobby of watching military airplanes and collecting their tail numbers. Polly had never joined the ranks of jet enthusiasts before, but she was the most interested observer present this evening.

She tried not to let herself worry, but the gusting winds frightened her. How could they fly in this awful weather? How dare they take chances with her Peter's life? She was being silly, she knew. The jet would never take off if the weather were outside its limitations; the aircrew had no wish to needlessly endanger their own lives.

At the end of the runway, the KC-135 slowly turned. Its engines wound up with a distinctive whine, then it began to move, slowly picking up speed as it passed Polly's vantage point. Far down the runway it became airborne, its landing gear folded away, and the noise drifted into a distant rumble. Polly watched it climb until it disappeared into the clouds. Her lips trembled; tears blurred her sight; her head ached. A long, gusting sigh finally escaped, turning into a sob. He was gone! She had hoped to make it to the military air terminal in time to see him once more; but when she spotted the Stratotanker on the ramp as she drove past the base, she knew she was too late. At least she had seen him take off; she could be thankful for that.

That week was the longest in her memory, and Thursday evening it became even worse. Driving home from work, she realized that not all the pain in her throat was caused by repressed tears. She did not feel well. Sure enough, by the time she went to bed, her temperature was over one hundred degrees, and her throat hurt badly. "Peter gave me something to remember him by," she muttered at her reflection in the mirror, then smiled ruefully. "I don't even mind sharing a virus with him!"

That night her illness kept her from dwelling on how much she missed her man, though she did shed a few tears before dropping off to sleep. The next morning she was awakened by a knock at her door. "Pauline? Are you in there?"

"Yes, Mum," Polly struggled to open her eyes. "What's wrong? You can come in."

Elaine opened the door, her gray eyes concerned. "It's after ten o'clock, Pauline. Aren't you working today? Is it an American holiday? You never sleep in this late. Are you ill?"

"Yes." Polly's reply was brief. "I feel awful. I called in sick today."

Elaine had never been an overly sympathetic person. "You'll feel better when you're up and about. I've invited guests in for contract this evening, and I must leave for work within the hour. If you would vacuum and do up the dishes, that would be smashing."

Polly groaned inwardly, but acquiesced. "I will, Mum, but I don't want to be here tonight. I don't feel like entertaining. I'll spend the evening at Peter's house. I can sleep all I want while I'm there." Other nights she had simply rushed in to feed the cat, then hurried home to fix dinner. It would be pleasant to sit back and relax in Peter's home, and feel close to him.

Wendell was touchingly glad to see her when she arrived that afternoon. He told her of his joy repeatedly, all the while weaving between her feet. Polly switched on the living room light and felt a wave of loneliness for Peter engulf her. His weight bench was free of clothing, the table held no cereal boxes, the shelves and desk were orderly. It was too clean, too cold, and too quiet. Polly turned up the radiator and popped a Keith Green CD into the stereo, trying to bring life back into the cottage. It helped. To the tune of "You Put This Love in My Heart," croaking lyrics she had memorized many years before, Polly wandered to the kitchen to feed Wendell.

Peter had stacked what appeared to be a year's supply of cat food and litter along the far wall beside the refrigerator. Wendell headed straight for it with an imperative meow, then purred noisily about her legs as she opened a can and dumped it into his bowl. She watched him eat, wondering how he could continue to purr while chewing and gulping. She decided to clean the cat box later.

Feeling thirsty, she opened the refrigerator. Peter had apparently visited the commissary recently, for she found a goodly supply of fresh fruit and bread. It would never keep until his return, so she helped herself to an apple and a glass of bottled water. After leaving the front door open a crack so Wendell could explore the garden if he wished to, she collapsed on the sofa, crunched her apple, and stared about the room. *This room needs a rug*, she decided, *and some pictures on the walls. I wonder why he doesn't have any?*

Wendell hopped into her lap, still purring like a buzz saw.

Polly wrapped the apple core in a paper napkin and lay down, petting the warm cat. He curled into the curve of her side and fell asleep. His purr kept Polly awake for a while, but she soon followed his lead and dozed off. Her dreams were wild, filled with visions of Peter, Kevin, Strike Eagles, and at last, a ringing bell. . .she struggled back to consciousness. The telephone! Should she answer it? Without further thought, she staggered to Peter's desk and lifted the receiver. "Hello?" Her voice started like a bullfrog's croak, then died out in a squeak.

"Polly?" The reply was hoarse, too, but easier to recognize as a human voice.

"Peter!" she squawked joyously. "How are you?"

"Fine, Honey, but you sound terrible! I guess you caught my bug, eh?"

"Yes, but it wasn't your fault. It's good to hear your voice." It was disconcerting to hear her own voice echo back each time she spoke. "How come I keep hearing an echo?"

"That's the way these satellite calls are; it's patched through from the base. I can only talk for ten minutes, so I'll try to make it good. I'm sure glad I caught you at my house. I tried yours first, then decided to try my place. How's Wendell?"

"He's fine, but lonely. We were sleeping on the sofa when you called. Peter, I was having the craziest dream! You were going to take me for an F-15 ride, only I had to sit on the wing. There was a seat belt on the wing and everything!"

He chuckled. "That's a new one. I wish I could take you with me, but I was thinking more on the lines of stuffing you into a travel pod."

"Wish I'd fit. Are you settled in there?"

"Yeah. I'm still tired, but I'll have the weekend to rest up. I'm not scheduled to fly again 'til Monday. Hey, by the way, can you break my racquetball date with Mike for tomorrow? I forgot all about it. Maybe he already knows I'm gone."

"Yes, he knows. I talked with Lisa the other night."

"Thanks. Polly, I want to ask you something before I forget. You know, there're all kinds of shops here with brass things and Turkish rugs and gold jewelry for great prices. I bought a few things for my family last time I was here, but I've never had a sweetheart to inspire a spending spree. What would you like me to bring you?"

"Peter, I have no idea! You don't need to bring me anything. I only want to have you back, that's all. Why don't you buy some things for your home? This room could use a warm rug and some decorations."

"Good idea! What colors, do you think? The rugs come in every hue imaginable."

"What colors do you want to use in your living room? Your sofa is neutral, so you could use whatever colors you like. How about blues, or a rich forest green?"

"Sounds great. I've never been much of a decorator, but I guess I'll get what I like and hopefully you'll like it, too. Ron Fry is picking up my mail on base; I told him to give it all to you. I'll mail any boxes to myself, but you feel free to open them and decorate the house with the contents. All right? Please?"

"I'd love to, Peter."

"Polly, I miss you something awful. I can still feel that kiss."

The phone lines must have transmitted the heat burning through Polly's body. As her knees gave way, she sank into a chair. "So can I."

"Did you mean that about giving me another when I return?"

"With all my heart."

"I'll want more, Polly. You know that, don't you?"

"What do you mean?" Her breath came short.

"When I return I'll be asking a certain question, and I'll need a prompt answer. You be thinking and praying carefully about your answer these next eight weeks, all right?"

"All right," she sounded choked. There was a significant silence.

"I'll call again next week, Polly; I'm only allowed one call a week. Thank you again for taking care of Wendell. Give him a rub for me, and tell him to give you a snuggle for me. Lucky cat!"

The warmth of his voice stayed with Polly for hours after she hung up the phone. Snuggling Wendell, she became involved in some of Peter's family photo albums, smiling over photos of him as a toothless first-grader, a rather pot-bellied schoolboy, then as a wiry teen with acne and a hairless chest. She carefully inspected the girls in several photographs, his dates to proms or church socials. Some of them had been very pretty. Peter had apparently not been the wallflower type. During his college years, one girl dominated the photos, a petite blond with a curvaceous figure and startlingly blue eyes. Polly pored over one photo of Peter and this girl—whose name was penciled on the margins of another photo as Stephanie—at a pool party. The girl's swimsuit had been modest, but she leaned against Peter's broad chest with an air of possession that sent steam from Polly's ears.

"This must be the one he nearly married," she concluded, her voice and expression hard with jealousy. "I wonder if he waited two months to give her a kiss. I bet she didn't let him!"

Mercifully, Stephanie soon disappeared from the photos.

The next several pages of the album were dominated by "hero shots" of Peter standing beside various jets; first a T-37 "Tweet," then a T-38 Talon, then an F-4 Phantom, and lastly an awesome F-15E Strike Eagle. In these photos Peter gradually matured from a fresh-faced college boy to the tough-featured man Polly knew and loved. The most striking changes had occurred over his seven-month stint in Saudi Arabia before and during the Gulf War. Stress lines had appeared on his face almost overnight, and his boyish grin was seen much less often in the album from that time on.

The most recent photo in the album had been taken more than a year ago. It pictured Peter in front of his cottage, probably taken to send home to family. Polly closed the book with a thoughtful frown marring her brow. It gave her an odd, lonely feeling to realize how long Peter had lived without knowing her. Would they complete their lives together, or would she be just another fleeting face in his photo album?

"I need to be getting on home," she told the cat, but he snoozed unconcerned. Lying back again, Polly reconsidered. Her mother's party might well run late into the night, and Polly had no wish to join it. She was comfortable here, safe and warm, and Wendell was enjoying her company. It was not a difficult decision. She closed and locked the front door, turned out the lights and the stereo, and headed upstairs. The cat followed her as though this were an everyday occurrence.

"Well, your dad did give me permission to stay here once in a while, and I don't see why tonight shouldn't be one of those onces," she excused herself to the cat. Peter's bedroom was tidy, the bed made with a crocheted afghan folded at its foot. To her unutterable delight, an envelope leaned against the pillow, addressed with her name. She wasted no time opening it.

Dear Polly,

Just a quick note to say I'm sorry I turned down your offer of housesitting so abruptly. You were kind to think of it, but my first thought was of Morris's offer to you—you know what I mean. I don't want there to be any question about our relationship in anyone's mind, as we are to ". . .avoid even the appearance of evil." I don't think it would hurt for you to stay with Wendell now and then, though. Only be careful about answering the phone late at night—you could give my folks a turn, should they call. I didn't get a chance to tell them about my changed plans, but I'll write to them soon.

You changed the bedsheets yesterday, so they're almost clean—only slept on once. The other set is still wherever you put it. Please consider my house yours; turn it inside out, if you like. I like to think about you among my things, such as they are. I've never made this offer before, but then I've never known a woman like you, Polly. I feel as if I'm leaving half of myself behind. I know I'm leaving my heart here, for you've stolen it. I won't demand it back, as long as you give me yours in exchange.

My packing went faster than I'd expected, so I have a few minutes to spare. There are

*many things I wished to tell you, but had no
time to say them. I plan to spend much time
studying my Bible while I'm away. I have
much to learn and no time to waste. Whenever you read a special verse or learn a
lesson from the Lord, please write and tell me
about it. I want to share these most important
things with you, Polly. Knowing and loving
you inspires me anew to be the man God
wants me to be. If I'm to be the head of a
home, I must be a Godly leader, and learn to
love my wife as Christ loves the church.
Loving you is not a difficulty (the difficulty
would be in not loving you), but I want my
love to have real depth—to be the kind that
lasts through thick and thin, sickness and
health. . .you get the idea. The only source of
that kind of love is God; I know that much.*

*It isn't a Bible verse, but I'm claiming that
adage, "Absence makes the heart grow
fonder." I'm scared to death you'll forget me
while I'm away, or that you'll find that your
feelings for me are not what they seemed, but
I must trust the Lord to "watch between me
and thee while we are absent, one from the
other." If you are the woman He has planned
for me, our love will only be strengthened
through our trials.*

*Brave words and true, but I must admit
I've begged Him on my knees every day for
two months now to let you be my wife. I can't
imagine ever caring for another woman the*

way I love you, Polly.
  *The taxi should be here any moment. Don't
forget me. I am forever*

Your P.S.

Clad in one of Peter's faded T-shirts, Polly slipped between the almost-clean sheets, still clutching her first love
letter from Peter. Wendell settled beside her and began
grooming himself, his rhythmic purr undisturbed by his
constant licking. Polly might have been irritated by the noise
at any other time, but tonight she was thoroughly distracted.
Before switching off the lamp, she nearly had Peter's letter
memorized.

twelve

"Beep-beep. Beep-beep. Beep-beep." The insistent alarm on Peter's watch penetrated his slumber. He rolled over and sat up, fumbling to turn it off. Blinking, scratching the back of his head where the hair stood up straight, he stumbled out of bed to switch on the light.

"Oh-dark-thirty," he grumbled, stretching up toward the ceiling, then reaching to touch his toes. A game of tennis the previous afternoon had left him somewhat stiff and sore. Minutes later he was in the shower, allowing the steaming water to slough away his aches and pains.

His small dorm room lacked beauty, but it was comfortable and private. An array of photographs lined the bedside table: Polly feeding pigeons in Trafalgar Square, her shoulders and arms lined with birds, a delighted smile on her lovely face; Polly and Peter in front of one of those enormous lions on the square, taken by an obliging Japanese tourist; a close-up of Polly taken without warning as she perused her menu in the dimly lit Mexican restaurant. Peter never tired of looking at them. They added a touch of beauty to the room.

Hair slicked, flight suit zipped up, boots laced, he tucked his wallet and I.D. in one chest pocket, his flight cap in an ankle pocket, and stepped into the hallway. As flight lead today, he would drive the bus to the Tab V aircraft shelters. At 6:30, he sat behind the wheel of the idling bus while another pilot and two Wizzos climbed in. "Glad you could show up today, Soup, Lay, Spike," Peter greeted them.

"Howdy, Pump," the other pilot returned his greeting, and Spike yawned, "Mawnin'."

"Yeah, right," was Kevin Morris's only response as he slumped into a seat. He had shaved, but his hair wasn't wet and one cheek was sleep-creased.

"Don't mind Lay; I had to pound on his door again this morning to drag him out of the sack. Pity me—I have to fly with him." Soup, whose real name was Dave Winters, leaned back in his seat, hands clasped behind his damp head. "When you goin' back, Kev? Tuesday?"

"No, I've got another ten days. Can't wait to get out of this dump."

It was a tradition in the squadron for each flight crew member to have a "Dupp" name—a sobriquet usually bestowed upon new flight crews during deployments, something like a fraternity initiation. Peter wasn't fond of his Dupp, "Pump," derived from his interest in weight lifting, but he figured it could easily have been worse. Some of the nicknames were embarrassing to their reluctant bearers, but all newcomers were eager to have a Dupp and be a true member of the squadron. Pete had described it to Polly as, "You know, a male-bonding thing." He was seldom called by his Dupp; most of his friends preferred "Shack."

Peter kept his eyes on the dark perimeter road that skirted Incirlik Air Base's 10,000-foot runway. This was the first time he and Kevin Morris had been assigned to the same mission at OPC, although Peter had been in the country for three weeks.

"Does anyone want to stop for breakfast?" After the security gate, Pete pulled up behind a Tab V shelter at Katie's breakfast shop. "Shop" was a generous description of the aluminum trailer on cement blocks. Katie's place wasn't fancy, but it was a godsend to hungry flight crews with erratic schedules, and the breakfast burritos were downright tasty.

"I'll get it." Still yawning, Spike hopped out of the bus and turned back to take their orders. After he slammed the door, Peter put the bus in gear and rumbled off to park at SOC 1. He was already thoroughly tired of this almost daily routine; the novelty had worn off quickly, hastened by his loneliness for Polly. He resolutely put her out of his mind during working hours, but she had a way of sneaking into his thoughts during any idle moment.

The four men checked the Air Tasking Order and got lineup cards from the Intel-NCOs. Spike soon arrived with their breakfasts. Munching his breakfast burritos, Peter added details and checked his information for accuracy. Each day an intricate and detailed schedule was distributed to every crew involved in OPC, listing American, French, and English aircraft, their flight paths and times, creating an immense and complicated choreography.

Captain Peter Shackleton would be leading a two-ship of F-15E Strike Eagles into northern Iraq for the purpose of protecting the Kurdish people from Saddam Hussein's army. United Nations air forces had been stationed at Incirlik Air Base in Turkey since the close of the Gulf War to enforce the northern no-fly zone. Although many Americans had nearly forgotten the Gulf War already, Operation Provide Comfort meant survival for the Kurds—the continuation of their race. Without this protection, these people would have been systematically eradicated from the face of the earth, and they recognized their debt with touching gratitude, though few of the men who protected them would ever meet a Kurd face to face.

The gravity of their job was reflected in the men's faces. Though often appearing immature or irreverent in ordinary

life situations, the pilots and Weapons System Officers took
their duty seriously. This was a war-time situation; although
their country was not officially at war, their mission could
be deadly. The Eagles were armed to the teeth, carrying two
external fuel tanks, laser-guided bombs, air-to-air missiles,
500 rounds of ammunition for the Vulcan cannon, plus chaff
and flares. The men loved to fly, but these $60 million jets
were not toys.

Pete and Spike arrived early at their jet, allowing plenty
of time to ground check it, then stretch and breathe for a
few minutes. Peter half-sat on the steel lattice of the Tab V
door to watch the sun rise behind an eastern mountain range.
Glorious color filled the sky, but on the ground there was
nothing to be seen but Tab Vs. A wave of loneliness hit Peter; he felt far from home. This part of his life could never
be shared with Polly. She could never understand what it
was like here, so different from the outside world.

"It's time," he stated, startling Spike out of a similar rev-
erie. They reentered the hangar. Ten minutes before engine
start time, thirty-five minutes before take-off, the two men
climbed up the tall ladder, carrying their helmet bags. Peter
always felt guilty about stepping on that brand new black
sheepskin seat with his dirty boots, but he had no choice.
After hooking his helmet bag's handle on the canopy bar
and slinging it over the far side of the jet, he sat down like a
king on his throne, looking down at the ground crew below.

At times Pete felt that his humanity disappeared when he
climbed into a jet, as though he were being absorbed into
the machine. He felt cut off from life on earth. There was
little time for reflection now, however. He buckled himself
into the ejection seat, then snapped his oxygen hose and
intercom hose into a fitting on his harness. Now he hauled
in his helmet bag, removing his helmet, pubs, and the Data

Transfer Module. He strapped one check list to his leg, arranged the other pubs, and plugged the DTM into its slot.

The great jet still lay dormant beneath him like a sleeping giant. Shackleton checked various switches and slipped on his helmet. He left his mask dangling until just before engine start, but rolled on his gloves. Behind him, in the back seat, Spike had also buckled into the jet, and on the ground below, the crew chief had been checking pins and panels, getting everything buttoned up and ready to go.

Time to start the jet. From the backseat Spike gave a thumbs up, then the crew chief gave a thumbs up. Peter pulled the Jet Fuel Starter handle. He could hear the hydraulic accumulator firing into the JFS; it began to spin up, and the jet came to life. The control panel began to light up; the communication system could now be used. Looking at the chief, Peter said, "Crank two."

"Fire bottles posted. All clear fore and aft. Clear to crank number two," the chief returned crisply. He wore a headset that plugged into the jet, allowing him to converse with the flight crew.

Peter started engine two, then moved the right-hand throttle forward into idle position, giving the engine fuel. He could hear it start to spin up. Now all panel lights were on; the jet was fully alive.

Though the men's ears were protected by their helmets, the reverberations from that incredibly powerful engine rattled their very bones. Peter glanced over both shoulders, then called, "Canopy clear," and moved the handle to the "lower" position. The great bubble closed over their heads, slid into position and sealed—then Pete locked it, protecting them from that tremendous noise. Now he and Spike were completely built into the airplane, separate from the earth.

He repeated the engine-start procedure for engine one, then finished turning systems on and testing them. As he ran manual and automatic tests the jet bucked and wiggled, demonstrating the hydraulic power of the stabs and ailerons.

Pete checked in Dave Winters, his wingman, who had been starting up his jet in another Tab V. Their call sign for this mission was Hitman. "Hitman, check aux," he called on the prebriefed auxiliary radio frequency, then released the switch. "Hitman, push seven aux. Hitman, check aux."

"Two," Dave reported, sounding more like "Toop" on the radio.

Pete called the mission director on the other side of the base, "Mad Dog, Hitman as fragged, looking for words." He was asking if there were last-minute changes to their assigned mission.

"No words, press."

"Incirlik ground, Hitman as fragged, taxi from India with the numbers."

"Hitman, Incirlik ground, taxi to runway zero five."

"Hitman."

The crew chief disconnected from the airplane and gave it one final check. At Pete's signal, the chocks were pulled from the wheels. The jet began to taxi out, marshalled by the crew chief until they reached the yellow runway lines. The other Eagle left its hangar and joined up behind.

At the India loop taxiway, they waited while arming crews pulled pins from their weapons. Job completed, the chief gave Peter a thumbs-up and a salute. Peter returned signal and salute, then waved to the crew before taxiing out of the loop to the north parallel taxiway. At the holding area just before the runway they stopped, and Peter began to call:

"Hitman, push three. Hitman, check." A radio frequency change.

"Two," the wingman's reply.

"Incirlik tower, Hitman as fragged, number one."

"Hitman, Incirlik tower, you're clear for take-off, change to departure. Have a good flight."

"Hitman's clear for take-off." Shackleton taxied out to the runway, taking the right-hand side. His wingman joined up, slightly behind and to the left half of the runway. Once in position, both pilots gave their jets a final check, then Captain Winters gave his flight lead a head nod, indicating that he was ready to go.

"Hitman, check."

"Two."

Peter gave a quick wave, put his hands on both throttles, pushed abruptly into afterburner, and released the brakes. The blowers started lighting immediately, giving an instant increase in thrust. A clear blue flame spewing golden shock wave diamonds was visible, extending twenty-five feet behind the jet as it rolled down the runway, accelerating rapidly. At rotation speed Peter pulled back on the stick to lift the nose, and at 180 knots the jet lifted off. Once they were airborne, he grabbed the landing-gear handle and lifted it. Looking over his right shoulder, he glimpsed the end of the runway below. Off the jet's nose appeared a ring of mountains and a bowl-shaped valley. Beyond the mountains was the Mediterranean Sea, and beyond the sea was Syria. At 350 knots, still climbing, he pulled the throttles out of afterburner and pushed them into full military power. Looking into the center mirror on his canopy, he saw the runway far below and behind. A little black dot visible between his jet's twin tails was the wingman, just now taking off behind.

He called, "Incirlik departure, Hitman as fragged on climb out, passing five thousand for two-seven-oh."

"Hitman, Incirlik departure, radar contact."

It was a beautiful day. "What a view," Spike remarked. "There's Snake Castle below. Have you been there yet?"

"No. Have you?"

"Yeah. It's worth seeing."

Peter ran the usual system and radar checks while they traveled; then the two jets spread about a mile apart and turned east. At fifty miles out they said good-bye to Incirlik and checked in with AWACS, the modified Boeing 707 carrying an enormous radar dome on its back. "Popeye, Hitman as fragged."

"Hitman, Popeye, radar contact," the AWACS replied.

During the forty-five minute flight to Iraq, Pete and Spike passed the time discussing various systems in their jet or catching up on personal news. Spike loved to talk about his children, and Pete always asked about them. "Becky pulled the fishbowl over on top of herself last week, Tanya says. Tanya rescued the fish, but two of 'em died the next day and Ron was furious. Says he'll never let Becky in his room again."

"It's not easy being a big brother. I've been there, and I know."

"So, how's it goin' with your woman? Serious stuff?"

"Yeah." Peter smiled, recalling that good-bye embrace.

Spike was silent for a moment, then, "You know, I hate to mention this, but wasn't she Morris's main squeeze?"

"Not anymore. She's all mine now."

"She's a babe—a real lady, too, I think. How'd you get her away from him?"

"I didn't. They broke up before I asked her out. It was all on the up-and-up." He glanced at his watch, "Time to check in, Spike."

Time to check in with "Baron," the man in charge of coordinating all flights in the Area of Responsibility.

"Baron, Hitman as fragged, looking for words."

"Roger, Hitman, Baron has you loud and clear. No changes. Press."

Peter began to feel keyed up. Iraq was dead ahead. "Hitman, fence in." They were now crossing into enemy territory. Both pilots armed their chaff and flare and turned on their radar-jamming pods. Time to look for bad guys.

Their first assignment was a fun one: flying low level through the mountains of northern Iraq. Whipping along through mountain passes, they glimpsed Saddam Hussein's palace—a wreck since the war—scudded over snow-capped peaks, glimpsed mud-hut villages, then exited the funnel of mountains at a lake and made a sharp right turn into a great plain. That mission accomplished, they then relieved a pair of F-15Cs that needed to refuel, taking over their job of patrolling the skies over Iraq. Flying in great circles, they would turn north to give themselves room, then turn "hot," facing south to look for enemies with their powerful radar. It was an uneventful Combat Air Patrol, and when the other Eagles returned, Peter took his two-ship to air refuel. Relaxing, they "fenced out," turned some equipment off, and searched for the tanker with their radar. The KC-135 Stratotanker traced great circles above snowy mountain peaks.

Spike looked around, enjoying the scenery while Peter joined up on the tanker. "Don't want to jump out here, Shack. It looks truly cold down there!" A four-ship of F-16s had just finished refueling as they approached. Peter flew directly to the boom while his wingman joined up on the tanker's right wing. He could see the boom operator's face peering through the window in the tanker's belly above his canopy. Peter maneuvered his jet into position, then the boom operator carefully inserted the long probe into the receptacle in the Eagle's left wing. On a windy day it could be unnerving to see the long, flexible boom waving about so close to the canopy. But the refueling went flawlessly this time, and soon Pete switched places with Dave, flying in formation with the tanker. It was a fabulous scene; the tanker appeared to float in the crystal blue sky while smaller jets buzzed above, around, and beneath it, like kittens teasing their dignified mother. Before Winters finished refueling, an EF-111 had joined up, waiting in line for his turn.

Later they did another Defensive Counter Air-Combat Air Patrol period. Another pair of jets, perhaps the same F-15Cs they had spelled earlier, patrolled the eastern half of the no-fly zone, while Shackleton's two-ship patrolled the western half. Pete listened to their radio calls, timing his sweeps so that his two-ship turned cold while the F-15Cs turned hot, and hot while they turned cold. This way one set of radars would always be watching Iraq. They identified other friendly aircraft with their radar, but did not lock on.

Several Iraqi jets circled two air bases south of the thirty sixth parallel, or "line of death," as the crews called it. Peter watched them in the radar, thinking how easily this boring patrol could turn into an "ugly furball" if those jets should decide to try their luck in the no-fly zone.

Just after turning hot for a second sweep, the radio crackled, "Hitman Two. Contact single group, Bullseye, 290 for 22." It was Kevin Morris, excitement quivering in his voice. "Five hundred feet, northbound hot." He believed he had spotted an enemy aircraft heading north into the no-fly zone.

From Pete's backseat, Spike replied, "Hitman One. Contact there, skip it. It's a truck." Peter grinned, hearing Spike's dry chuckle over their private radio, "I knew he was gonna call that. All these new guys call the trucks out."

Not long after this minor adventure, Pete received a call from Baron: they were to return home thirty minutes early.

Peter obediently headed for the drawbridge and fenced out.

During their flight home he ran an ops check, then told his wingman to rejoin for a battle-damage check. They checked each other's jets from all angles, then Shackleton took the lead again and made a pushing motion with one hand. Winters obediently rolled out to one mile away.

Peter called Baron and announced their return to base with "Baron, Hitman's RTB."

The deep voice with a southern drawl replied, "Incirlik's calling ten thousand scattered, unlimited visibility. Runway zero five is the active. Have a nice trip home and see ya later."

Peter squirmed uncomfortably in his seat, longing to get off his backside. Spike brought up their former subject. "Did you know Morris has a picture of her in his room?"

"No, I didn't know."

"Are you sure he knows they're broken up?"

"Yes, I'm sure he knows."

"Okay, it's your life."

To Peter's relief, Dave broke in on the radio, "Hitman Two on the aux. Hey Shack, looks like we got some F-1s joining up with us from low six."

"That's okay. Just keep going straight and level, let 'em join and we'll get some pictures of 'em."

Two French Mirage F-1s appeared from below, one on Pete's left, the other sliding between the two Eagles.

"Mind if I come in for Kodak?" Dave inquired.

"You're cleared Kodak." This gave the wingman permission to fly wherever he wished in order to get good pictures. Morris could be seen in the backseat of the other jet, his camera at the ready.

The French pilots quickly realized they were on camera and closed into tight formation until Kevin had finished. Then, with a casual wave, they climbed out, obviously trying to be cool and leave the Strike Eagles behind.

Dave growled, "Hey, they're trying to beat us!"

"Roger," Pete responded eagerly, "Let's see what we can do." The two Eagles climbed up to 41,000 feet, traveling at .95 Mach.

"Wish we didn't have these rotten bombs on so we could go faster. They're getting away," Morris complained bitterly.

But then, "Look, they're slowing down!" Spike was jubilant.

Peter was no calmer. "I think they're out of gas. We're gonna win!"

Boyish whoops and cheers crackled over the radio as the French jets fell far behind.

At eighty miles out the Eagles began their descent and switched their radios from Popeye, the AWACS, to Incirlik arrival. The two pilots let their jets down gradually, clearing their approach with radar and the control tower. Just as the runway came into sight five miles to the right, they received a call from Incirlik arrival. "Hitman, keep your speed up if you can. Got some Mirages coming in behind you that are short on gas."

"Hitman, willco." As soon as Peter stopped transmitting, both flight crews burst into laughter. "I told ya we ran 'em out of gas!"

Relaxed and cheerful, the pilots made their turns and came in to land. Peter timed his landing perfectly while Spike waved his arms wildly in the backseat. The WSO hadn't lost his mind—each landing was graded by a "judge" at SOC 1 for the pilot's smoothness and the WSO's original wave!

The two Eagles were already taxiing down the north parallel toward India loop when the Mirages landed. Both Eagle crews indulged in cheers and catcalls, just for the fun of it!

thirteen

"Where for lunch?" Pete asked as they climbed into the bus. "Anyone want to stop at Katic's again?"

"No way. I want some real food. How about Frank's Franks?"

"Oh, yeah, like hot dogs are real food," Kevin scoffed at Spike's suggestion. "I'm for the O'Club."

Putting the bus in gear, Pete made his decision. "I'll go back to the dorm, and we all can walk to lunch where we like."

No one argued, but Dave brought up the question, "How about dinner tonight? I vote for Rose's."

"I'm in the mood for Italian food myself," Kevin objected. "I can't stand another chicken-cheese tava. It's Friday, anyway. Party night."

"I want to shop at Copper Ali's, so I vote for Musdat's or Rose's," Spike sided with Dave.

"I could go for a Rose's Special," Peter agreed, "and I have shopping to do. Want to look at rugs with me, Spike? I hear you have a collection."

Spike grinned modestly. "Tanya says I have good taste. I recommend the silk-on-silk Harakas, if you want top quality. My wife says I could go into selling rugs if the air force releases me."

"I just want something that looks good and wears well. I'm not into spending top dollar for something to walk on." Peter parked the bus in front of the dorm and pocketed the keys.

"Meet for dinner at five-thirty?" Dave suggested. "I'll call the cab. Sorry Lay, maybe we'll go for Italian next time."

Kevin shrugged. "It don't matter."

Back in his room, Peter showered and changed clothes, then sat down with Bible in hand for his quiet time. He was hungry, but wasn't in the mood to walk across the base for a meal. Spike's comments about Polly ate at him. Did Kevin Morris know about his relationship with Polly? Did Kevin still consider Polly his girlfriend? Pete knew about the scene in the Mildenhall Officers' Club, but perhaps Kevin considered that incident a simple lovers' quarrel and expected to iron out the relationship upon his return to England. Otherwise, why would he still display her photograph?

His eyes lifted to his own photos of Polly, and the ache in his heart grew more intense. She was so incredibly beautiful! Perhaps he had only been fooling himself, imagining that a woman like Pauline Burns would want to marry ordinary, run-of-the-mill Peter Shackleton.

Returning to his open Bible, he stared at the page, trying to read, but understanding nothing. Finally, he screwed his eyes shut and pounded his fist on one knee, groaning, "Lord, what am I supposed to do? Go talk to him? I don't have a clue what to say. I hardly know the guy!"

He sat on the edge of his bed for several minutes, forehead resting on both fists. "God, I'll try to talk to him, but You'll have to give me the right words. Please give me the power to. . .to love him, to see him the way You see him. Time for 'Operation Provide Power,' Mike would say. As far as Polly and I are concerned, Your will be done. I've said that before, but I guess this is a test of my sincerity. It doesn't hurt to ask, though, so—I sure do want her for my wife! Amen." Smiling ruefully, he pulled on running shoes and left the room.

Kevin answered his knock with a surprised look, "Hey, Shack, what's up?" His hair was damp, like Peter's, his feet bare. "Come on in."

Glancing around the neat room, Pete saw the blown-up photo of Polly on Kevin's bedside table. She posed on a sandy beach, wearing shorts and a tank top, her hair blowing in the wind. Morris was a good photographer, and his subject matter. . . Wow! Following his gaze, Kevin remarked, "You know Polly, don't you?"

Pete lifted one brow. "Yeah, I sure do. That's what I came to talk about, Lay."

"Well, have a seat there. I'll sit on the bed."

Kevin Morris was an all-right guy, really—no worse than most. Peter respected the man as a fellow officer. Morris lacked experience as a WSO, but he was learning fast and worked hard. Pete wanted to find fault with him, but Morris was no villain. To make things worse, even Peter could see the attraction the man would have for women; Kevin was too good-looking for his own good. His proposition to Polly had been wrong, but he had probably made it with the best of intentions—according to modern moral standards. Still, there was the matter of the stories he had told. . . With these thoughts running through his mind, Peter fumbled for words. "You, uh. . . Have you heard that I'm dating Polly?"

Kevin's smoky blue eyes searched his face. "Yeah, I've heard. I'm not sore; she did break up with me."

"I made sure she was free before I asked her out."

Kevin nodded. "Every man for himself. I. . .uh, well, how are things going? I mean, with you here and her there?"

"I call her once a week and we both write, but I don't like being so far away."

"I don't either. I've thought about calling her, but I know I'm not ready yet."

"What do you mean?"

Morris shook his dark head soberly. "I've been thinking a lot about why I lost her, Shack. I'd like to believe it was her fault, but I know better. She's too good for me, that's all."

Peter's eyes were opened. Before him sat a lonely man, young in years but old in bitter experience, handsome in looks but miserably selfish at heart. A wave of understanding sympathy washed over him. How the Spirit yearned to fill this man's empty life! "It's not that she's too good, but that you aren't allowing God to have His way in your life, Kevin. You say you're a Christian, but no one would know it from your actions and words. Polly could never be happy with that sort of compromise. Don't you know her better than that?"

The other man was silent for a long moment. "You're right, I know, but it's not what I want to hear right now."

"One more thing. You need to take back the crude lies you spread about her. You know as well as I do that Polly's a lady. She was crushed when she heard what you'd been saying about her."

Morris winced. "I'm sorry she heard about that. I was drunk and got carried away. . . All right, I'll take it all back. I don't ever want to hurt her again." His voice was quiet, actually humble. "Shack, do. . .do you think God would still want me?"

Again Peter felt the Spirit's prompting. "I'm sure He does. Read the parable of the prodigal son and First John chapters one and two if you doubt His forgiveness."

Morris nodded. "Thanks."

Peter rose, "Kevin, I need to tell you straight out: I plan to ask Polly to marry me when I return to England."

The two men locked eyes, measuring one another. "I've

asked her already, but she's got this thing against pilots and WSOs. I'm considering getting out after this tour. If Polly would marry me, it'd be worth giving up this job. I love that woman."

Pete's heart constricted, but his voice was calm. "So do I. Well, see you at dinner."

Peter spent most of the afternoon walking around the base, thinking and praying. He knew he had done the right thing, but almost wished he hadn't done it. His trust in Polly was great, but his self-confidence wavered under pressure. Kevin Morris the arrogant jerk had been weak competition, but Kevin Morris the repentant, committed follower of Christ could be a serious rival for Polly's affections. Furthermore, Morris would soon be back in England to press his suit, while Peter languished in Turkey for six more weeks. Polly had pledged fidelity, yes, but she might honor her promise not to see other men while he was away, then request her freedom upon his return. The thought turned his stomach. He almost skipped dinner, but decided at the last minute that too much solitude was bad for him.

He was waiting with the other men when their taxi drove up the street. "Right front!" Peter claimed. It was the custom for flight crews to share a taxi and take a chance on paying the fare.

"Left front!"

"Right rear!"

"That leaves left rear for me," Dave figured. The accepted method of deciding who would pay for the cab was to choose a tire as the car approached; when it stopped in front of the restaurant, the tire with the air tube closest to the ground lost.

It was a five-minute drive through the base, out the main gate, then along the pot-holed road between knick-knack stores. In front of Rose's the cab came to a stop, and the men hopped out to check their tires. "Three o'clock," Spike said.

"Five o'clock," Peter sounded discouraged.

"Twelve o'clock," Kevin was smug.

Dave's was at seven o'clock, so the others inspected the tying tires carefully, and the decision went Dave's way. Peter accepted their judgment philosophically; he hadn't paid the cab fare for nearly a week.

As soon as the fare was paid, they were overwhelmed with welcome. A swarm of men from the restaurant half-dragged them inside, reeling off the unchanging menu in sing-song voices, "Chicken tava, cheese tava, beef tava, lamb chops. . ." Peter lost track at that point. The red carpet treatment was unnerving at first, but enjoyable once you got used to it, and the food was excellent. Glancing around the small room, he experienced a familiar wave of home-sickness. *This place would be a blast, if only Polly were here with me*. He had a horrible feeling Morris might be thinking the exact same thought.

After dinner they split up. Dave and Kevin headed toward the Falcon Club, an American-type bar, where they might stay for many more hours. Peter and Spike walked down the street toward Copper Ali's, running the gauntlet of hopeful restaurant owners and shoeshine boys. "Shoeshine, *habib*? Shoeshine, *habib*? For you, twenty-five cents. I make them shine!"

Peter looked down at the bright-eyed boy, not more than seven years old, and shook his head. "But I'm wearing tennis shoes."

"No matter, for you," the boy insisted, trailing behind them as they continued down the street.

Shopping for rugs with Spike was an experience. The

salesman knew Spike on sight, called him by name, and brought out the finest carpets for Peter's inspection. Peter felt rather guilty as the friendly Turk rolled out carpet after carpet. All this work, and he hadn't really intended to buy anything tonight! One carpet caught his eye, however, a machine-made carpet in rich shades of green, blue, and tan. "That would look good in my living room," he remarked.

Walking out of the store, hefting an unwieldy box over one shoulder, he shook his head in awe. "How does he do that?"

Spike grinned knowingly, but asked, "Do what?"

"Get people to buy a carpet when they didn't intend to. My wallet is considerably lighter."

"Oh, come on, you bought a cheap one! You're just getting your feet wet. You've gotta get one of the handmade ones before you can talk of a light wallet. Coming to Copper Ali's with me?"

"If I can fit through the doorway with this box."

Peter resisted temptation at the brass and copper shop, though he noted several attractive items for future reference. Spike was ready to return to the base after this stop, so the two called a taxi.

"Gonna call your wife tonight?" Peter asked as they settled back in the car's hard seat.

Spike shook his head. "Not 'til tomorrow. She takes the kids out for dinner on Fridays when I'm away. Saturday is our day. You gonna call your girlfriend?"

"Yeah. Friday night's our night. She stays at my house to keep my cat company and waits for my call. By the way, I talked with Morris this afternoon. He knows about Polly and me."

"And?"

"Says it's every man for himself."

"You're hoping to marry her?"

"Soon as she'll have me," Pete confessed with a grin. "It ain't easy to convince her over the phone, though."

"No, these separations are rough. At least she'll know what she's in for. Tanya hates it, but she sticks with me."

❧

The telephone patch-through always took a while. Peter waited anxiously, hungry for the sound of Polly's voice. At last she answered, her low, slightly husky voice having its usual melting effect on him. "Hello, Polly. I can't tell you how good it is to hear your voice!"

They had learned to talk quickly during these treasured conversations. Silence was a waste of valuable time. Mundane topics were saved for letters, but greetings and assurances of love were indispensible.

"Did you fly today?"

"Yeah, I flew with Spike Sykes, Dave Winters, and Kevin Morris this morning. Not much happened, but that's good news. I'm flight lead tomorrow morning, too. How've you been doing? Keeping busy?"

"Yes. What with teaching the girls' club, attending Bible studies, and helping direct the Christmas program, I don't have time to sit around and feel sorry for myself. Sometimes I can't help thinking how much more fun everything would be if you were with me, but I try not to dwell on it."

"I know what you mean. I keep thinking this place would be like a resort if you were here. Without you it resembles a prison."

"I need a hug, Peter. I really do! I hug Wendell a lot, but he doesn't hug back."

"Crazy cat! Wish I could trade places with him. You just make sure you don't satisfy that hug need elsewhere. I'll spend days catching up when I get there, all right?" He could almost feel her firm softness in his arms. His eyes closed at the pang of desire.

"Mmm, sounds good to me. My need couldn't be satisfied by anyone but you, Peter." Elated by the urgency in his voice, Polly sounded more sultry than ever.

"Whoa-ho, time to change the subject, woman. I've gotta sleep tonight, you know."

"Do I keep you awake nights, Peter?"

He winced, letting out a mirthless chuckle. "If you only knew."

"What do you dream about?"

"Polly, I mean it. Please change the subject."

"I'm only teasing, Peter. You're not angry, are you?"

"I'm sorry. I'm not in the mood to joke about things like that."

"Don't be mad at me, Peter! I just miss you so much, and . . .and I want you to miss me. Sometimes I wonder if you find me very attractive."

This time he snorted. "Polly, that's the silliest thing I've ever heard! I told you before, I haven't so much as looked at another woman since I first laid eyes on you. Being away from you is. . .torture. All I can think about is your kiss, how you felt in my arms. . ." He groaned, "Polly, don't do this to me."

"But I feel ridiculous when I remember how I had to ask you to kiss me! And I initiated our first hug, too. How do you think that makes me feel?"

"Polly, try to understand. I love you. I want to marry you. I've never asked another woman to marry me. Maybe you think I'm a cold-blooded chump, but I've only been trying to—Oh, never mind!" He slumped against the wall, rubbing his burning eyes.

"No, no, I know you're not cold-blooded! I. . .I don't know

why I said all that," she gasped. "I just. . .I want you to hold me!"

Peter pinched the bridge of his nose. "Polly, please don't cry."

"I don't mean to," she choked, "but you sounded so fed up with me."

"Not with you. Never with you. I hate trying to explain myself over the blasted telephone, that's all. Polly, I'm almost out of time—thirty seconds left. Is everything all right there? You're well and have all you need?"

"I'm all right, Peter, except for missing you. I love you so much, and. . . You fly careful and miss me lots." Her plea ended in a sob.

"No trouble keeping that promise. 'Bye, Polly."

Eyes hard, jaw clenched, he slowly walked back to his dorm room, speaking to no one, and scooped the closeup shot of Polly from his bedside table. His ravenous eyes devoured her features: wide-spaced, slightly slanted eyes under arching brows, full red lips that smiled so easily, high cheek bones beneath creamy skin, rounded chin and dainty neck, and the strong nose that somehow only augmented her beauty. He caressed the photographed cheek with one rough finger, trying to recall its softness. An inarticulate plea, half-sob, tore from his throat, and he fell to his knees beside the bed.

fourteen

Oncoming headlights dazzled Polly's eyes, and the deluge of rain further obscured her vision. Driving at night always frightened her, and in this weather her fingers gripped the steering wheel until they ached. She was tempted to go straight home from work and let Wendell wait until tomorrow for his supper, but the thought of that lonely kitty waiting trustingly for her at the door spurred her on.

It was Monday of Thanksgiving week, and Polly could hardly wait for her holiday. She planned to spend Thursday with the Drays, and Friday she would talk with Peter again. Since that emotional conversation a few weeks back, their calls had been slightly stiff and awkward. It wasn't that they cared less for one another, Polly assured herself. It was simply a natural result of their separation. When he returned, all would be right again. His short letters still arrived regularly, about three a week, but Polly had fallen behind in her correspondence. She often thought of what she would say when next she wrote to him, but her pen seldom found its way to paper.

Peter's cottage was dark when she pulled in to park behind the Vauxhall. At that moment, Peter himself seemed like a remote memory, a pleasant but distant dream. Reality consisted only of his empty house and hungry cat.

"I hope you appreciate this," she grumbled, then stooped to caress the rumbling animal at her feet. "I hope he appreciates it, too. Oh, Wendell." Her voice caught. "It seems so long since he went away. I wonder if things will be the same when he returns!"

Her loneliness prodded her to pull down the photo albums again and brood over Peter's likeness. The sight of his face brought a lump to her throat. It looked like him, down to the dear crinkles around his eyes and the cute upward curl at the edges of his mouth—but the picture lacked his warmth, his tenderness, his touch. A wave of longing swept over her—longing to be held in his arms, to quiver at his breath against her skin, to hear his heartbeat beneath her ear. . .

She closed the album and replaced it on the shelf. "Wendell." The cat regarded her with serious amber eyes. "It will be three more weeks until he returns. Can I last that long?"

Leaving the dark cottage behind, she sent her mini splashing along back lanes toward home. Not far from the highway she hit something in the road, and a moment later the little car shuddered and began to flounder. Polly's heart turned to ice. "What's wrong?" Stopping the car, she stared through the streaming windshield. "Lord, please help me out of this!"

Grabbing the penlight she kept in the glove compartment, she stepped into inches of water and studied her situation. Even her unmechanical eye could spot the problem: her left front tire was totally flat.

Hoisting her umbrella higher, she cast about for a solution. She could attempt to change the tire herself in the pitch dark in the mud, or she could hike back to Peter's cottage and telephone for help, or she could hike back and wait until morning to call for help, or. . .she ran out of ideas at that point. None of these ideas appealed to her. The cottage was at least two miles back, and her pumps were not built for hiking. It probably would be wiser to walk to the nearest house and ask to use the telephone, or. . .she suddenly brightened, remembering a small pub that stood at this road's junction with the A11. It could not be more than half a mile from where she stood, and it would have a public telephone.

She was drenched, shivering, frightened, and feeling thoroughly sorry for herself by the time she approached The Hare and Hound. The red telephone box beside the car park was occupied, and she waited under the pub's dripping eaves for the man to finish his call. "Lord," she muttered quietly, "I don't know what You're trying to teach me through this experience, but I want to learn the lesson quickly! Please help me find someone who can change my tire, or at least give me a ride home!"

The thought of a taxi had occurred to her, but a quick inspection of her finances quashed that idea. She didn't know if taxis took personal checks, but she wasn't willing to chance it, and a sum total of seventy-five pence reposed in her coin purse. Enough for a few phone calls, but not enough for taxi fare home.

At last, the call box was empty. Polly folded the door shut behind herself and dialed the Drays' number. No answer. She called home; same response. Desperately thinking up the numbers of various church friends, she tried to call them, but to no avail. She opened the telephone book, searching for names of other friends, then she called the church to see if the pastor might be there, but no one could be found to help her! She closed the book with a snap. "God, this isn't funny! This is impossible! How can all those people be away from home, talking on the telephone, or have no car this evening? It's not fair! What can I do?" Tears began to trickle down her nose and moisten the dog-eared telephone directory. "The only person I haven't called is Kevin Morris, and I can't call him."

Leaning against the cold side of the box, she folded her arms and sulked. "So, should I just stand here, waiting for someone to come help me, or what? Where is my guardian angel when I need him? Why does Peter have to be thousands of miles away right now? It's not fair!" She slapped at the glass door, receiving no satisfaction from her outburst.

"All right, I'll call Kevin, but he won't be home either—or else he'll laugh at the idea of helping me!" Dialing the number with vicious punches at the buttons, she waited angrily while the phone rang.

Just as she moved to hang up, he answered, "Kevin Morris speaking."

"Kevin!" she gasped, then floundered. What could she say? "I. . .uh, this is—"

"Polly! My darling, you have no idea. What an answer to prayer!"

She was floored. The tenderness and exultation in that heart-stealing voice took her completely by surprise. Fumbling for words, she finally blurted her request, "Kevin, I've got a flat tire and I'm stranded at a pub on the A11. Can you give me a ride home?"

Some of the thrill left his voice, but he still dazed her with overflowing thoughtfulness, "Of course I will, Polly. Tell me exactly where you are, and I'll come for you."

When Polly hung up the telephone, she felt slightly sick inside. What would Peter think about this mess? She had promised him not to see other men, but this was not a date or social outing. Still, she had a sneaking feeling that she might have found another solution had she looked harder.

Polly watched for Kevin at a front window of the pub, avoiding the smoke-shrouded warmth of the bar. The sight of his silver Corvette brought back memories, not all of them unpleasant, and Polly could not sort out her emotions as she climbed into the front seat and pulled the door shut. "Thank you so much, Kevin. I was truly at my wits' end. I have no money, and my mother isn't home!" Her soaked pumps left muddy streaks on the car's immaculate carpeting.

He didn't drive away immediately, but sat looking at her in the pub's spotlight. She squirmed under that ardent gaze. "Polly, I can't begin to tell you how good it is to see you again, and to have you beside me in my car. I was beginning to think it would never happen. I'm glad you thought of me when you were in need."

Her thoughts must have shown on her face, for he remarked, "You aren't happy to be with me, though, are you?"

"That's not it, exactly, Kevin. I just feel guilty that you think. . . It sounds ungrateful to say this, but I only called you because I couldn't get anyone else." She dropped her eyes, half expecting, half hoping to be put out of his car.

He was silent, so she glanced up. The expression on his face sent a jolt through her heart. "Thank you for being honest, Polly." He put the car into gear. "It's undoubtedly kinder in the long run. I was foolish to hope for more."

The car flowed effortlessly over the highway, flashing past other vehicles as though they stood still. Polly struggled for conversation, but could think of nothing to say. Kevin filled the void, "I want you to know something, Polly. I've lived a lifetime in these last few months, since the day I realized I'd lost you. Not until that realization hit me did I know what a treasure you were—a treasure I had valued lightly and deserved to lose. I know there isn't much chance for me anymore, but I want you to know that I've turned my life over to God. I accepted Christ when I was a kid, so I've always considered myself a Christian, but my life didn't show it, as you know. I thought all Christians were more or less like me—until I met you and some of your friends. I thought you must be fake, because no one could really be that good, but now I know your goodness comes from the Lord, not from any special 'holy' quality in you. What's more, I can have that same goodness in me."

He paused to collect his thoughts, flashing her a quick glance. Her wide eyes stared through the windshield with something like fear in them. "Polly, I want to apologize again for insulting you, lying about you, and two-timing you. I also want to thank you for shaking me out of my illusions about Christians. If you had given in to my demands, who knows whether I ever would have turned to God? It all hit me one day down in Turkey, what I'd done, and why I'd lost you. I talked with Pete Shackleton about God. You know him, don't you?"

"Yes, very well. Did he tell you about me? I mean about dating me?"

"Yeah, and it just about killed me—the jealousy, I mean. I've been miserable ever since we broke up, Polly. I guess it was God showing me what a louse I am, I don't know, but I couldn't take it, and didn't know where to turn until Shack confronted me about not living my faith. I've been meeting with Chaplain Carson since I came back to England, doing a Bible study. I'm no saint, Polly, and I can never undo the past, but from here on out I'm God's man."

He parked in front of her flat and turned to find her eyes fixed on his face. "I'm very happy to hear it, Kevin." She looked more puzzled than pleased.

"Is it really too late for me? I still love you, Polly. More now than ever before. I've been seriously considering going into the ministry, believe it or not. My dream was to become a pilot, and ever since I washed out of flight school

I've been carrying a chip on my shoulder, trying to prove to the world how tough I am. That's another burden God has lifted from me: I don't resent pilots anymore, because I realize now that God's plan for my life is the one that'll satisfy me, not my plan. If he wants me to remain a WSO, then that's what I'll do, but if you want me to get out of the service, that seems to me to be a clear sign from God that I should get out. I'd do anything for you, Polly."

The longing, the humility in his deep, rich voice nearly broke Polly down. When he reached for her she backed away, one hand on the door handle, the other held out to ward him off. "I don't know what to say, Kevin! I'm honored, but. . .I don't know what to say." Her voice trembled dangerously.

"I wanted to call you as soon as I returned from Turkey. I picked up the phone more than once, but God told me to wait until you called me, and He gave me the strength to wait. When I heard your voice tonight, I knew my prayer had been answered. I know you're confused, Polly—this is sudden, and you haven't had time to sort out your feelings. Because I love you so much, I'm willing to wait. I know—I just *know* beyond all doubt—that God planned all along for us to marry."

Afterward, Polly could not remember how she climbed out of his car. The next thing she knew, she was facing Kevin on the front step. The rain had lightened to a misty drizzle, creating a glistening halo around the street lamps and frosting Kevin's dark hair with tiny beads. Feeling intensely awkward, Polly blurted, "Uh, thank you very much, Kevin. Good-bye." She unlocked the door, but he pulled her back to face him.

His eyes gleamed in the porch light. "I'll change that tire for you in the morning, Polly. I have a late show time. I'll take you to work first, then pick up your car. Say, can we have Thanksgiving dinner together?"

"Thank you, but I already have plans."

He sucked in his full lower lip and chewed on it for a moment—a mannerism she remembered well. "How about dinner tomorrow night—no, make that lunch; I'm flying late. How about it?"

Polly's lips parted, then shut. How could she refuse him when he was being so kind to her? "I. . .I can't, Kevin."

He looked disappointed, but not crushed. "All right. Maybe this weekend, then. Good night, Darling." He turned away, then turned back. His eyes flared, and before she could protest he had swept her into his arms and crushed warm, demanding lips against hers. Polly could not help being stirred by the contact, but into her mind flashed the memory of a photograph of Peter Shackleton embracing a gorgeous blonde siren. She had felt betrayed by that picture taken many years before—how would Peter feel if he could see her this very moment?

With a strength of will that startled both of them, she pushed Kevin away—*hard*. "No! No, I'm sorry, but I can't . . .I can't do that, Kevin." She turned to go inside, but he grasped her arm.

"I'll be here in the morning, Polly."

"Yes—No—Oh, I don't know! Just go away!" She wrested her arm away and almost slammed the door behind herself.

☙

Far away in a quiet farmhouse in Illinois, Bill and Linda Weston had just snuggled down on their sofa to watch National Velvet when the telephone rang. "Now who can that be?" Linda frowned, extricating herself from her husband's arms.

"Shall I pause the tape?" he asked rather sleepily. Bill

seldom saw more than the first ten minutes of any movie.

"All right. I'll hurry," his wife called back from the hallway. Bill pushed a button on the remote control and rose to put another log on the fire. A moment later he pricked up his ears.

"Polly!" his wife was saying, "Whatever is the matter? Are you hurt? Or is it Elaine?" Within moments Bill was at her side, pushing the button to allow a conference call. Polly's voice filled the hallway.

"I'm.all right, Mama Lin, and so is Mum, but I've got a problem, and I had to call you. You weren't asleep or anything were you?"

Bill recognized borderline hysteria in his niece's voice. "No, we weren't asleep," he assured her. "It's only eight-thirty here, but it must be two-thirty in the morning there, Angel. Why are you up so late?"

Polly latched on to his voice like a lifeline. "Oh, Papa Bill, I can't sleep! I've been tossing and turning for hours. I desperately need to talk to you."

"Well, now you have us. What is the trouble, Darling?" Linda cast anxious eyes at her husband, but kept her voice calm.

"I'm so confused! I don't know what to do," her voice broke, and for a moment they heard nothing but sobs.

"Polly, control yourself and tell us the story from the beginning," Bill ordered firmly. White lines circled his set mouth. "Does this trouble have to do with that man you've been seeing?"

Polly took an audible breath. "It has to do with both men I've been seeing, Papa. I haven't written for so long, I can't remember what I told you."

"We know that you broke up with the Weapons System Officer, and that you've been dating a pilot who embodies all the virtues. Has he let you down, too?"

"No, no, it isn't his fault. He's away in Turkey, and has no idea what's going on here." Polly quickly brought her relatives up to date on the latest romantic developments in her life. ". . .and Kevin says it's God's plan for us to be together, and now I'm horribly confused. What is God's will for me? Is Kevin right, and God planned this entire thing so that we could marry? Or is he wrong, and Peter is the right man for me?"

Linda looked up at her husband with question marks in her eyes. He lifted straggly gray brows at her, but took charge. "Polly, were you confused about your feelings for Peter before you saw Kevin tonight?"

"No, I was absolutely sure I would marry Peter when he returned from Turkey. . .or at least I thought I was sure. Now that I think about it, would I have called Kevin tonight if I didn't still have some feelings for him, some lingering doubts? Maybe God directed me to call him in answer to his prayers. I just don't know!"

Linda took over. "Honey, do you want to marry Kevin, and you're sad because you must break Peter's heart? Or are you sad because you feel you should marry Kevin, but you don't really want to?"

Silence. She tried again, "Polly? Tell me how you felt when Kevin kissed you tonight. Was it immediately obvious to you that you were mistaken about Peter and had really loved Kevin all along?"

"No. . .Oh, Mama, it's hard to put my feelings into words! I felt. . .I felt excited, I guess. . .I mean, it's flattering to have him so crazy about me, willing to give up everything to marry me. . .but when he kissed me all I could think of was how hurt Peter would be if he could see me kissing another man. I mean, I promised him not to see any other men while he was away, and there I was, letting Kevin kiss me! I feel so jealous at the idea of him kissing another woman. . ." The voice on the line faded away.

"Polly." Bill tried to keep his amusement out of his voice. Tell me, Angel: which man do you really want to marry?"

"Peter." She sounded like a very little girl.

"Then what's all this fuss about? Your Peter sounds like a far better catch to me. I mean, this Kevin fellow *might* turn out to be a great man of God someday, but it sounds to me as if he needs time to grow up. Are you willing to marry him now and take the chance that he won't grow up, or do you want to wait around for several years to make sure before you marry him? Angel, the man has only just turned his life over to God; do you give him credit for knowing God's will for your life better than you do?"

They waited patiently for her to digest this idea. "Papa Bill, I feel like a first-class idiot! You're right—as always. I've been thinking with my hormones again."

Bill chuckled. "That's my Angel."

Linda smiled and hugged her husband. "Polly, has Peter actually proposed marriage to you?"

"Yes, in a way, though he hasn't asked for my answer yet. He's supposed to be back in three weeks, and it still seems like forever!"

"So, what are you going to tell him? Do you think you can endure these separations, Honey? It won't get any easier after you're married. He might be off fighting a war when your first child is born, or miss the baby's first birthday. You'll handle plumbing failures, assorted household disasters, insurance and mortgage problems, and who-knows-what-else all by yourself. You'll spend lonely nights in a cold bed wondering what your man is doing on the other side of the world. It's not an easy life. Your mother couldn't handle it."

"What do you mean? I know it was hard for her, but she did stick with Dad."

"Polly, we haven't told you this because it wasn't something you needed to know before now, but your mother wrote a 'Dear John' letter to your father just before he was shot down."

"Oh!"

At Polly's agonized gasp, tears clogged Linda's throat. She looked to her husband, and Bill completed the story. "When they brought her the news of his death, Elaine had a complete nervous breakdown and nearly lost you, Angel. We and your grandparents flew to England to be with her, and she signed you over to us when you were born. For years we heard nothing from her, but when you were twelve years old she wrote, asking about you."

"I remember how strange it felt to fly to England to visit a mother I had never known." Polly's voice was dreamlike. "No wonder Mum acts so strangely about my father. She believes her letter made him die, doesn't she?"

"Yes, but I hope time has eased the pain for her somewhat. It wasn't easy for us to let you go to her this last time, Polly, but we knew it was the Lord's will. She is your mother, after all, and she has no one but you, since her mother died. Her second husband was not good to her. It was almost a blessing to her when he passed away, though he left her nothing."

"She's seeing a dear man now, Mama Lin. His name is Wilfred Timms, and he is good to her. I've wondered, at times, if he might be a believer. He attends his Anglican church faithfully, though he's shy of speaking about spiritual things. I think he'd marry Mum in a moment if she gave him any encouragement."

"Perhaps if you marry, Elaine might accept him; you never know," Linda pondered. "The poor dear needs someone to love her. We all do."

"We'll keep her in our prayers, Angel," Bill promised, "and you and Peter, too. Polly, you're a very different woman from your mother, and I believe you could handle marriage with a military man, especially since you have the Lord's help. I don't want to convince you to marry anyone—that's your choice—but if you really love the man, don't let self-doubt stand in your way. You have more than you've ever given yourself credit for, girl."

Polly's voice was small, "Thank you, Papa Bill."

"Now, you'd better get to bed. You have to work in the morning, don't you? You find someone else to help you with your car; make no mistake about that. A promise is a promise, and don't you forget it! Your Peter has enough pressures on him without your adding to them!"

"Yes, Papa. Good night! I love you both and miss you more than I can say. Oh, and Happy Thanksgiving. I probably won't talk to you again soon."

"Thank you, dear. You have a nice holiday, too. We always miss you. Oh, one thing more," Linda interjected. "Don't you dare marry without giving us a chance to be there, all right?"

"I can't promise, Mama, because it might depend on Peter's schedule, but I'll do my best. Get those passports ready!"

Bill chuckled. "Hear that? She already sounds like a first-rate military wife—good and flexible. Make no promises you might not be able to keep! That's my girl."

"Good-bye, Polly darling!"

"'Bye. I love you!"

fifteen

"Polly, would you come stir the gravy while I carve?" Lisa requested over one shoulder.

Her friend immediately complied, inquiring, "Why doesn't Mike carve the turkey? Oh, Lis, that bird looks fabulous!"

"He is handsome, isn't he?" Lisa sharpened her carving knife, giving the golden fowl a proud glance. "Mike doesn't know how to carve a turkey, or so he says. I think he just prefers to keep out of the kitchen. Polly, are you ever going to tell me what happened with Kevin the other night? Now's as good a time as any."

Polly looked harassed. "I'd rather tell you after dinner, Lisa. I'm sure I'd ruin something if I tried to tell you now. I can't talk and cook simultaneously."

"All right, I'll give you a reprieve. Too bad your mom didn't join us today; we have enough food here for an army. She could've brought her boyfriend along, but maybe they would have felt awkward with all us Americans."

"They had reservations to eat at the White Hart this evening, but it was very kind of you to invite them. Mum was touched."

"Kevin Morris tried to wangle an invitation to dinner out of Mike, but Mike was inhospitable for the first time in my memory! Thankfully his soft heart didn't get the better of him. I'm so glad you asked Mike to change your tire instead of letting Kevin do it." Lisa arranged tender, steaming slices of white meat on her china platter.

"I am, too. It was good of Mike to do it for me, and Vicky

kindly gave me a ride to work. So, it all worked out all right, in the end."

"Is it the end?"

"I sincerely hope so. Lisa, this is thickened. Do you have a gravy boat? I'll pour some in. Is the table completely set?"

"Yes. Would you carry in the yams and the corn? I'll get the turkey, stuffing, gravy, and the fruit salad."

"Don't you do mashed potatoes?" Using a crocheted pot holder, Polly pulled the casserole dish of candied yams from the oven.

"No, Mike doesn't like them, and I've gotten out of the habit. Hope you don't miss 'em!" Lisa followed her to the dining room, bearing a loaded platter. "Mike, dinner's ready. Can you get the children ready?"

"Sure." Mike excused himself from the other guests, two very young single airmen from his shop.

Back in the kitchen, Lisa reopened the subject. "Has Kevin called you again?"

Polly dropped hot rolls into the basket, her face cloudy. "Yes. He won't give up, Lisa. I don't know what to do."

"You've told him how it is with you and Peter?"

"I told him that I promised Peter not to see other men while he was away, and that we have a serious relationship. If only I had told him so Monday night!"

"He doesn't want to believe it?" Lisa held the gravy boat with both hands, loath to leave the kitchen until her curiosity was appeased.

Polly shook her head, staring down at the rolls. "He's so sure I'll marry him that it frightens me! When I try to discourage him, he smiles this long-suffering, superior smile and reminds me that God's will is always best. As though I were rebelling against God by refusing him!"

"Did Mike tell you that Kevin showed up to change your

tire even after you asked him not to?"

Polly stared. "No! What happened?"

"He arrived just as Mike was putting the jack away and he was real nice and friendly, but Mike could tell he was displeased. He wanted to play the shining knight and help you out." Lisa's little smile told Polly that she was enjoying herself.

"It's not funny! I feel as if I opened Pandora's box when I called him that night, and I don't know how to put him back inside."

"He's too good-looking to be an imp, but I know what you mean. At least you have 'Hope,' just like Pandora."

"What do you mean?"

"Peter will be home soon. I don't think he'll allow Kevin to retain illusions about your relationship for long."

"Oh, I hope not!" Polly closed her eyes, fighting back tears. "I'm so frustrated and lonely for Peter! Please don't make me talk about Kevin any more. I don't even want to think about him."

"All right, Sweetie. You know what? I think you should be thankful, really. If you had any haunting doubts about which man you really love, they should be laid to rest forever now. Come on, let's eat before Mr. Turkey gets cold."

≈

Friday night, Polly waited longingly for Peter's weekly call. The burning desire to hear his voice ate at her emotions, giving her a hollow feeling inside. She selected a leatherbound volume of *Ivanhoe* from his shelves, curled up on the sofa with Wendell in her lap, and tried to lose herself in the story. In her imagination, Sir Wilfred of Ivanhoe took on Peter's features, while Sir Brian DuBois-Gilbert was Kevin, blue eyes and all. To Polly's dismay, she found herself identifying with the luckless Rebecca, doomed to be DuBois-Gilbert's woman or belong to no one at all, while Ivanhoe's beloved Rowena bore a remarkable resemblance to golden-haired Stephanie, Peter's old flame.

It was well after midnight when Polly suddenly awoke, finding the book open upon her chest where it had fallen. She sat up, answering Wendell's reproachful look with a heartbroken wail, "He never called!" Sleepy and depressed, she allowed the tears to flow freely as she prepared for bed, wearing Peter's oldest T-shirt and yearning for him with every fibre of her being. Her heart cried out to the Lord, and she finally fell asleep, comforted only by His everlasting arms.

❧

Gray circles underlined Polly's eyes, but she worked with unabated determination. Her fingers flew over the typewriter keys. The other secretaries speculated about her love life, but asked no questions, figuring she would share when she was ready. It was the first of December, and she had not spoken to Peter for a week and a half. His letters still came, but they were shorter than ever, telling only about his flights, the funny stunts pulled by some of his friends, or describing some trinket or rug he had sent home. They were all signed with love, but Polly found them dissatisfying. Her one consolation: he had sent her a gorgeous black leather jacket for a Thanksgiving gift, therefore he must not have completely forgotten her! Polly wore it everywhere she went, rather like a security blanket.

The telephone on her desk rang, and she picked it up, answering mechanically, "Current Ops, Polly speaking."

Her own voice echoed back, then Peter spoke, "Polly? I'm sorry to bother you at work, but I had the best chance of catching you there. I couldn't get a telephone all weekend. Are you busy?"

"Peter! I'm not too busy to talk to you. I've missed you terribly." The tears that seemed always near the surface these days filled her eyes yet again.

"I've missed you, too." Comforting words, but Polly felt a lack.

"Is something wrong? Are you all right? You don't have to stay there over Christmas, do you?" The worst possibility she could think of.

"No, I don't. I might even be home early. Nothing has changed on my end, but I'm wondering about you. I got a letter from Kevin Morris the other day."

"You did?" A pause. "W-what did he say?"

"Do you want me to read it to you?"

His expressionless voice cut at her heart. "No, of course not. Peter, I don't—"

"It seems his heart was overflowing with praise to the Lord and he felt constrained to share his joy with me. After all, the Lord used me to bring him back 'into the fold.' He told how he had been praying that God would give you back to him."

Polly opened her mouth, but he went on relentlessly. "His hopes were fulfilled when you called upon him to rescue you, but of course you know all about that. He made a particular point of telling me how wonderful it felt to hold you in his arms again."

"Oh, Peter, it wasn't like that! I only called him because I couldn't get anyone else—no one was home, and I had no money for a taxi! I'm more sorry than you'll ever know that I called Kevin. I should have hiked back to your house through the dark and rain and mud and waited until morning, I guess, but at the time calling Kevin seemed the best thing to do!"

"Yeah, and giving him a kiss seemed the best thing to do afterwards." Now Polly heard the jealousy in his suppressed voice.

Her temper reared its head. "I did not give him a kiss! He

took me unawares and stole one. I don't imagine he told you that I pushed him away and told him no, did he? I don't break my promises, Peter Jacob Shackleton, no matter what you think of me! Kevin has called me every day since then, asking me out and insisting that he'll be patient, since he's sure God intends me to marry him. He's driving me crazy, and the only hope in sight for me is that you'll return home soon and prove to him that I mean what I say!" Polly's trembling voice broke down, and she sobbed hysterically.

An officer with gold leaves on his shoulders walked into the office, looked at her with widening eyes, and backed out again. Vicky stared at Polly from her desk, then turned slowly back to her work.

"Polly," Peter tried to regain her attention. "Polly, calm down. I only have a few more minutes to talk to you! Please, Sweetheart. . .Polly, I'm sorry I doubted you. Listen to me, please? I shouldn't have doubted you, but you haven't been writing much, and I thought. . . I mean, I felt like maybe you were forgetting me. Oh, Polly, I hate being so far away from you!" His anguish and frustration reverberated over the wires. "You can be sure I'll let Morris know how serious I am as soon as I get there. I want my ring on your finger and your name signed on our wedding license before my next deployment, understand? No more doubts about whose woman you are!"

Polly's heart swelled; her breast rose and fell rapidly. "I understand. I. . .oh, Peter, come home quickly!"

His voice was deeper than she had ever heard it. "If I had my way, I'd be flying out today. Wait for me, Polly. I'll try to call you Friday; I've got to hang up now. Good-bye, Sweetheart."

"I love you, Peter!" Her voice echoed back, then he was gone.

sixteen

Two days later Polly had a visitor. Captain Fry dropped by her office as she covered her typewriter, his grinning, freckled face bringing an answering smile. "Miss Pauline Burns?" As though he didn't know.

"Hello, Ron. Any packages for me, delivery boy?"

"One or two. Say, how'd you like the rug Pete sent? Did you put it on the living room floor?" He leaned against the door jam.

"Yes, and it brings life into the room. It's amazing! Peter will be pleased. He really has good taste."

"You sound surprised," Ron teased.

She chuckled, picking up her purse. "Well, I'll admit a doubt or two. What has he sent this time?"

"I'll let you find out. By the way, I have a message for you." The skinny pilot's sky blue eyes twinkled with mirth. "Pete sent word that you are to be at the squadron tomorrow afternoon at fifteen hundred hours."

"I. . .here? Why?" The truth hit her with a jolt that made her stagger. "He's coming home tomorrow?"

"Yup. Leading a two-ship with Spike in his backseat, Yeager and Malone in the other jet. I'll drive you out to the hangars. Sound good?"

Her glowing face was his answer.

Polly arrived early at the squadron Saturday afternoon, but one wife was already there with her two adolescent children. "Hello, I don't think I've met you," the attractive woman greeted Polly with a smile. "I'm Janice Malone, and these are Marie and Bryan."

Polly returned the greeting and introduced herself, "I'm Polly Burns, Pete Shackleton's girlfriend."

The Malone children played foozeball in the Panther Pub while the women sat around on cold vinyl sofas and talked. Rhonda Yeager, a young newlywed, remembered Polly from First Friday. Tanya Sykes had two school-age children and an energetic preschooler. Her husband, Spike, had been a WSO in the F-111 for three years before transferring into the F-15E, and Tanya had fascinating stories to tell about her husband's experiences in the Gulf War. "Becky was born one week before George left for Saudi, which wasn't easy; but one girl in the other squadron had her first child while her husband was bombing Iraq, so I don't dare complain."

Polly admired the woman's accepting attitude, but Tanya shrugged, "You have to enjoy the good times and make the best of the hard times, Polly. If you marry Shack, I bet you'll be a good wife. You look like the kind that sticks."

At 2:45, Ron Fry stuck his head into the pub. "They'll be landing in ten minutes, Ladies. Ready to ride out and watch?"

They piled into the back of the van, and Captain Fry drove them toward the field. He looked back over his shoulder, his irrepressible grin bringing color to Polly's cheeks. "Excited, Miss Burns?"

She nodded, feeling self-conscious. Her cherry red turtleneck, black stirrup pants, and glossy, free-flowing curls were for Peter's benefit, but she couldn't prevent other men from looking, and their admiration embarrassed her. Her fidgeting fingers buttoned up her black leather jacket then unbuttoned it several times during the short drive to the flight line. Mercifully, the drizzling rain stopped as they climbed out of the van.

The roar of jets accelerated her heart rate, and she saw her excitement mirrored in the eyes of the other women. Two gray Eagles approached the runway directly. "They're doing an instrument approach," Ron explained. "The weather isn't good enough for a landing pattern." Polly watched the lead jet touch down smoothly, coasting on its rear wheels before the nose slowly dropped and the front wheel touched. The speed-brake, a large panel on top of the fuselage, lifted to decrease the Eagle's speed. Polly could see two helmeted heads through the bubble canopy. "Nice landing," Fry muttered. "Show-off."

Polly grinned at him, then watched the jet until it taxied out of her sight. The other jet also landed smoothly, but to Polly's biased eye its touchdown lacked finesse. "Okay, ladies, we'll take you to the hangars now."

They dropped Mrs. Yeager and the Malones at one hangar, then drove on to the hardened aircraft shelter where Peter's jet would be parked. It was a huge, reinforced concrete structure, curved like an immense Quonset hut, with mechanized steel blast doors. Fry handed out packages of ear plugs before the jet approached. "You'll be needing these."

They stayed well away from the hangar while the jet parked. Conversation was impossible above the ear-piercing shrill of jet engines. The intense noise vibrated deep within Polly's body, making her grateful for the ear plugs. She watched in fascination as the ground crew attached cables to the idling jet and towed it carefully backward into the shelter. The two men in the cockpit were looking backward over their shoulders, checking to make sure the wings did not graze the sides of the shelter. Finally, the engines shut down. The silence was deafening.

Ron led the women and children into the hangar, where

they could stand at a distance and watch the men finish shutting down the aircraft. Polly waited beside Tanya while Captain Fry moved away to talk with some of the ground crew. Ladders were wheeled into place. The aircrew began to unstrap and unbuckle themselves from their ejection seats. Peter swung his helmet bag out onto the ladder and stood up. Looking out toward Polly, he gave a little wave. His hair was sweaty and tousled.

Sykes climbed down first. His wife and children ran to meet him, leaving Polly alone and fretting. Her breath came hard and fast. She felt suffocated, and unbuttoned her jacket for the fourth time since leaving the squadron. Peter stepped onto the ladder. Polly felt like fainting with suspense by the time he reached the bottom step. His narrowed eyes scanned her face as he approached.

Five feet away he stopped and set down his helmet bag. Now she could see that his face was colorless, tense, his cheeks imprinted in the shape of his oxygen mask. The layers of rubber "poopysuit," flight suit, G suit, and harness he wore added to his remote appearance.

"You came." His arms slowly reached out to her. "Polly?"

Then she was in his arms, feeling his cold, rough flight suit beneath her cheek, its metallic smell mixed with the odor of sweaty pilot, hearing the rush of Peter's breath and his relieved groan, "Oh, Polly!" His arms were exactly as she remembered them, strong and demanding, and she lifted eager lips for his kisses, stroking his cheeks and hair with trembling fingers.

Ron Fry elbowed the crew chief in the ribs. "Look at that!" he grinned, but a wistful envy touched his eyes.

Peter could hardly let go of Polly long enough to complete the walk-around inspection of his jet and retrieve his duffels from the travel pod. "Don't go anywhere," he

ordered gruffly. Life and vitality pulsated from him, in startling contrast to the exhausted figure she had seen alighting
from the jet only minutes before. "Polly, I had forgotten
how beautiful you are." The promise of more kisses in his
gleaming eyes, which roamed over her face and figure with
unaccustomed boldness, made her feel shy, but exhilarated.

She watched him check his jet, moving somewhat stiffly,
which could only be expected after sitting down for so long
in the cramped cockpit. His power of concentration impressed her; in spite of her presence he paid close attention
to his job, signing forms and talking with the crew chiefs.

At last they climbed into the step van and drove to the
debrief. Polly and the wives and children waited in the van
while the men went inside to answer questions about their
flight and fill out time cards. Excitement and tension made
Polly's hands clammy, her smile too bright, but the other
women weren't noticing. Peter seemed almost a stranger to
her, so professional and important. She suffered from a touch
of hero-worship, amazed that such a man could care for an
ordinary woman like herself.

Back at the squadron, the flight crews went into the life
support shop to change out of their g-suits and poopysuits.
The wives followed their men, and Polly joined them re-
luctantly. The men changed at their lockers, out of view,
while the wives laughed and giggled together, discussing a
recent party. They seemed entirely at ease, but Polly was
uncomfortable in the intensely masculine locker room environment. She stood by the door, wishing Peter would
hurry.

His face appeared around a row of lockers. "You can come
over here if you like. I'm decent."

She found him seated on a bench before his open locker.
He was bare-footed, wearing his flight suit, having removed

the poopysuit and liner from beneath it. His front zipper was halfway down, showing an expanse of white undershirt. He stopped stuffing equipment into his duffel and glanced up at her, "I'll be ready to go in a minute. Thanks for coming to get me, Polly."

"My pleasure," she admitted. "I would've been hurt had you asked anyone else to take you home." She picked up his scarf and twined it around her own neck.

"Yeah? I wasn't any too sure."

"You can be sure." She slipped behind him and began to massage his shoulders and neck. His undershirt was damp, but she cared not a whit. The muscles beneath it were smooth and hard.

To her delight, he closed his eyes and slumped his shoulders, groaning, "I'll give you a year to quit that."

She glanced around at the rows of lockers, each one decorated with a panther patch. "It's fun to see where you work." Splaying her hands over his chest, she pulled him backward in a possessive hug. "Being here makes me feel like. . .like part of you. I want to belong here."

His hands came up to grip hers, but at that interesting moment Rhonda Yeager appeared around the lockers, still talking to her husband over one shoulder. Polly straightened up instantly, and Peter released her, returning to his packing with outward nonchalance.

Later Polly hoped she had made her farewells to the other families with some degree of politeness, but at the time she was too absorbed in Peter to care. There was a kind of constraint between them, an awareness that tightened Polly's nerves.

Peter loaded his bags into her mini, noting the boxes Ron Fry had delivered. "Guess we'll have some fun unpacking, eh? Didn't expect to race those packages home." He slumped into the passenger seat and buckled in, turning to watch her with disconcerting hazel eyes as she slipped behind the wheel. Those big shoulders took up more than his share of the car's cramped interior.

"Would you like to drive?" She offered the keys.

He shook his head. "Been driving since early this morning. I'm more than happy to let you drive." Before she could turn the key in the ignition, he laid a hand on her arm. "Wait."

Turning slightly apprehensive eyes upon him, Polly asked, "Did you forget something?"

"No. . .I can't wait any longer, Polly. I hope you don't hate me forever for proposing in a parking lot, but—will you marry me?"

Polly's tension vanished into thin air. Confidence and that delightful sense of power took its place. A slow smile curved her red lips, and she gave a blatantly flirtatious flutter of her eyelashes. "Yes, as soon as possible!"

His eyes widened. "Polly, are you teasing me, or do you mean that?"

She reached out to run her fingers through the hair over his brow, suggesting, "I don't have plans for my Christmas holidays, do you?" Sliding her arms around his neck, she leaned shamelessly against his shoulder. "Lisa would slay me if I missed the Christmas program tomorrow night. But I have next weekend open."

He seemed immobilized by her touch. "Are you sure, Polly? I couldn't bear it if you were sorry later. Kevin Morris is—"

She was halfway into his lap, nuzzling into his neck and savoring the reactions her touch produced. "Peter, I have never been more sure of anything in my life!" Now she was completely draped across his lap, cradled in his arms, her fingers taking liberties with his hair and ears. "I do not love

Kevin Morris; I love you, and if you don't kiss me immediately, I. . .I think I'll die!"

His kiss left her craving still more. But he glanced out the windshield, then grinned down at her. Polly stopped stroking his rather stubbly cheek and gave him an affronted glare. "What's so funny?"

"The Yeagers, the Sykeses, and the Malones are getting an eyeful, Sweetheart." Polly turned in his arms—and colored to the roots of her hair. The other families were climbing into their nearby cars, smiling with amusement. It was dark outside, but the mini's front seat was floodlit by the squadron's spotlights. Spike gave Peter a thumbs-up and a cocky grin that made Polly want to slide under the dashboard. She immediately resumed her proper seat and started her car with a protesting rasp from the starter. "Easy, now. Settle down. Don't forget your seatbelt." Peter still grinned. She maintained what she hoped was a dignified silence until the base's main gate showed in her rearview mirror.

"So." Peter's fingers tangled themselves in her hair, wreaking havoc with her concentration. "How about if we have a talk with your mother tonight? Or do you want me to call your uncle and ask his permission?"

"But Peter, you need to get some sleep. You must be exhausted."

"I couldn't possibly sleep until we get this decided. I want a wedding date set and a honeymoon site planned and reserved before I turn in tonight. I'll call my parents and my little sis. Jeanie and Vic might be able to come for the wedding."

"My aunt and uncle might come, too. I warned them to get their passports ready, and if I know Papa Bill, he got to work on it the very next day. Where do you want to go on our honeymoon, Peter?"

"Somewhere private."

Polly smiled bashfully, but rushed on, "I mean, do you want to stay in this area or travel? We could fly to Majorca or someplace like that."

"Save Majorca for another time. I'd rather go to a nearby hotel for our honeymoon. No more than a few hours' drive. Would you mind?"

Polly heaved a relieved sigh. "I hoped you'd say that! I know the very place."

"And where is that?"

"It's an old mill that's been converted into a bed-and-breakfast down in Kent. We could go sight-seeing if we wanted to, or just stay around the hotel grounds. It's an easy drive from here, too, so we could come home for Christmas."

"You're serious about next weekend, aren't you?" Peter's eyes twinkled.

"Yes, aren't you?" Polly's smile faded.

"We might have to wait two weeks, Sweetheart, if you want family to be here. It could still be a Christmas wedding, though."

"Well, all right. But no longer than that!"

seventeen

It was the perfect setting for a honeymoon. The eighteenth-century mill house had been expanded and updated with enormous bathtubs, queen-sized beds, and thick carpeting throughout, but the ambience was strictly Old World. From the guest lounge, huge bay windows looked out upon an expanse of green lawn dotted with ancient oak and beech trees and bordered by a gently flowing brook. Logs crackled upon the open hearth; a grand piano played romantic big band music and Christmas carols in the afternoon hours; exquisite meals were taken at small private tables set with fine china and silver. Polly and Peter believed themselves in heaven for five luxurious days.

When the rain let up for a few hours the honeymooners walked across the lawn and along the stream bank, holding hands, heedless of the icy wind and drab scenery. A few ducks quacked hopefully in the water below, and Polly obliged them with some crumbled scones saved from breakfast. "They look cold, Peter."

"No colder than we are." Peter watched Polly's face, framed by the hood of her parka, his eyes soft though his voice was dry. The wind had whipped roses into his wife's cheeks and nose, and her eyes sparkled with life. "Having fun, Sweetheart?"

"More fun than I ever dreamed of! I never want to go back to reality. Can't we just stay here together forever?" Brushing crumbs from her fingers, she climbed up the shallow bank to his side.

"I don't think the U.S. government would approve. Otherwise, I'd be all for it." He wrapped one arm around her waist and pulled her close. "Want to walk further, or are you ready to go in?"

"Oh, let's walk a little longer. It might be raining again later, and I'm enjoying the fresh air. The way I've been eating this week, I'll turn into a butterball if I don't get some exercise."

Linking arms, Peter fell into step beside her. "Can't have that; I've got to carry you over our threshold in a few days." They walked in silence for a moment, then he observed, "We'd better head home early tomorrow if we want to get a Christmas tree." Silence again. "You're very quiet."

"I was thinking about our wedding. It was nice of all those people from the squadron to come. We had a much larger crowd than I expected, with air force people, Mum's friends, church friends, and our relatives."

"Kevin Morris looked heartbroken." Peter gave her a sidelong glance.

"Nonsense. He'll get over it."

"I hope he doesn't turn away from the Lord."

"If he does, then his faith wasn't worth much. Peter, I would never have married Kevin. He doesn't mean anything to me anymore; I only pity him. He has such a messed-up life! It'll take a miracle to straighten that man out. I'm not sure if even he knows when he is sincere and when he's putting on an act."

"I believe he is sincere, and anyway, God can do miracles. He did one in me: I survived those last few weeks of TDY without going mad. I've never been on an emotional roller-coaster like that before, and I don't care to repeat the experience!" He gave a crooked smile, but his eyes told her how true this confession actually was. "God used that time to build my faith, Polly. I had to learn to surrender you entirely to Him. By the time I came home, I was prepared to accept whatever came. Maybe I'm a pessimist, but I could hardly believe that you really wanted me."

She snuggled closer. "I know what you mean. I felt the same way about you."

They soon turned back toward the hotel. Polly brushed a dried leaf from her husband's shoulder. "I hope our relatives are enjoying England. I feel bad about abandoning them right after they got here."

Peter grinned. "I don't. They didn't expect us to stick around and entertain them, Polly."

She rolled her eyes, smiling shyly. "I know, but you know what I mean. I wish I could get to know your sister better, and I wish you could get to know Papa Bill and Mama Lin."

"We'll all get better acquainted on Christmas Day. That'll be quite a crowd in our little cottage, what with your mother and Wilfred too, but I'm glad they're coming."

"I hope they'll feel comfortable together, especially Mum and Mama Lin. I wish Mum would share her thoughts and plans with me. She's been withdrawn ever since we announced our engagement."

"Do you think she might marry Wilfred now?"

"Maybe. She's so lonely, Peter! I wish she would turn to the Lord for love and comfort, but she won't even let me talk about Him anymore."

"These things can take time, Sweetheart. We'll keep on praying for her and loving her, and who knows what God will do? You'll have lots of time to talk with her on Christmas Day, since Jeanie and Vic volunteered to prepare the dinner. You won't have to do a thing all day *except* talk."

"Spoiled rotten, that's what I'll be. Jeanie and Victor were so kind to take care of Wendell for us. I hope it didn't tie them down too much, having to watch our house."

"They planned to do local trips, anyway, like Cambridge and Newmarket. It was a fair trade, I think, the use of our mini in return for some kitty-sitting. They'll venture farther afield after the holidays. Nothing much is open right now, anyway."

"I hope Papa Bill and Mama Lin had better weather for their week in Wales than we had here."

"Weather? Has the weather been bad?"

Polly couldn't repress a smile, giving him a demure look from under her lashes. "You're right, it hardly mattered. I wouldn't have noticed a typhoon or a blizzard."

Pete grabbed her arm, turning her to face him. "Look at me like that, woman, and you'll get what you're asking for," he warned, putting words into actions. His nose felt like ice against her cheek, but his lips and hands were warm and remarkably reviving. Even Polly's half-frozen feet felt toasty by the time that kiss ended.

She nuzzled into his neck. "I think I've had enough walking for now, Husband."

"Mmm, I like the sound of that. Let's go, Wife." Holding her hand in his, he tucked it into his pocket, keeping her close to his side.

A duck, huddled on the bank with its beak under one wing, opened one eye to watch the young couple cross the wide green lawn and disappear into the hotel.

A Letter To Our Readers

Dear Reader:

In order that we might better contribute to your reading enjoyment, we would appreciate your taking a few minutes to respond to the following questions. When completed, please return to the following:

Rebecca Germany, Managing Editor
Heartsong Presents
P.O. Box 719
Uhrichsville, Ohio 44683

1. Did you enjoy reading *Eagle Pilot*?
   ❑ Very much. I would like to see more books
      by this author!
   ❑ Moderately
      I would have enjoyed it more if _____

   _____

2. Are you a member of **Heartsong Presents**? ❑Yes ❑No
   If no, where did you purchase this book? _____

   _____

3. What influenced your decision to purchase this
   book? (Check those that apply.)

❑ Cover	❑ Back cover copy
❑ Title	❑ Friends
❑ Publicity	❑ Other_____

4. How would you rate, on a scale from 1 (poor) to 5
   (superior), the cover design? _____

5. On a scale from 1 (poor) to 10 (superior), please rate the following elements.

    ___Heroine   ___Plot

    ___Hero   ___Inspirational theme

    ___Setting   ___Secondary characters

6. What settings would you like to see covered in **Heartsong Presents** books?_____

_____

_____

7. What are some inspirational themes you would like to see treated in future books?_____

_____

_____

8. Would you be interested in reading other **Heartsong Presents** titles? ❑ Yes ❑ No

9. Please check your age range:
  ❑ Under 18 ❑ 18-24 ❑ 25-34
  ❑ 35-45 ❑ 46-55 ❑ Over 55

10. How many hours per week do you read? _____

Name _____

Occupation_____

Address_____

City_____ State_____ Zip_____

Comfort FOOD

Ellen W. Caughey

Welcome to the kitchen of *Comfort Food*, a warm inviting space where tantalizing aromas mingle with the sage advice of Scripture, where low-fat foods are not a mélange of mysterious ingredients, where pride of family recipes is as fulfilling as the looks of satisfaction after a relished repast.

Welcome to a hearty collection of soups, main dishes, and desserts that stand ready to satisfy every comfort-seeking appetite. Includes 29 recipes that will make you feel right at home. 64 pages, Hardbound, 5" x 6 ½"

·········· Presents ··········

Great Inspirational Romance at a Great Price!

Heartsong Presents books are inspirational romances in contemporary and historical settings, designed to give you an enjoyable, spirit-lifting reading experience. You can choose wonderfully written titles from some of today's best authors like Veda Boyd Jones, Yvonne Lehman, Tracie J. Peterson, Nancy N. Rue, and many others.

When ordering quantities less than twelve, above titles are $2.95 each.

Hearts♥ng Presents
Love Stories Are Rated G!

That's for godly, gratifying, and of course, great! If you love a thrilling love story, but don't appreciate the sordidness of some popular paperback romances, **Heartsong Presents** is for you. In fact, **Heartsong Presents** is the *only inspirational romance book club*, the only one featuring love stories where Christian faith is the primary ingredient in a marriage relationship.

Sign up today to receive your first set of four, never before published Christian romances. Send no money now; you will receive a bill with the first shipment. You may cancel at any time without obligation, and if you aren't completely satisfied with any selection, you may return the books for an immediate refund!

Imagine. . .four new romances every four weeks—two historical, two contemporary—with men and women like you who long to meet the one God has chosen as the love of their lives. . .all for the low price of $9.97 postpaid.

To join, simply complete the coupon below and mail to the address provided. **Heartsong Presents** romances are rated G for another reason: They'll arrive *Godspeed!*